I0645748

Kink So Real

Mistress Amazon Reinvented and Other Stories

A Novel by
Gloria G. Brame

Moons Grove Press
British Columbia, Canada

Kink So Real: Mistress Amazon Reinvented and Other Stories

Copyright ©2024 by Gloria G. Brame
ISBN-13 978-1-77143-607-6
First Edition

Library and Archives Canada Cataloguing in Publication
Title: Kink so real : Mistress Amazon reinvented and other stories /
a novel by Gloria G. Brame.
Names: Brame, Gloria G., 1955-, author.
Identifiers: Canadiana (print) 20240426916 | Canadiana (ebook) 20240426924
| ISBN 9781771436076 (softcover) | ISBN 9781771436083 (PDF)
Subjects: LCGFT: Linked stories. | LCGFT: Novels.
Classification: LCC PS3602.R36 K56 2024 | DDC 813/.6—dc23

Artwork credit: Front cover artwork © Sumo - @designerbeauty
https://www.fiverr.com/designerbeauty

Moons Grove Press is an imprint
of CCB Publishing: www.ccbpublishing.com

Moons Grove Press
British Columbia, Canada
www.moonsgrovepress.com

Dedicated to all chosen families
who find shelter and power in love

≥ Contents ≤

∾ Chapter 1 ☙

AMAZON REINVENTED

Either life reinvents us or we reinvent ourselves. Jax chose the most radical path of all: to become who she was. She transformed her nature into her destiny. She tenderly nurtured it until kink was her normal. She filled her life by building a family of the heart. In helping them, she helped herself. She became their Matriarch and they became her fortress. Inside the walls, she planted a garden of love and all shared in the harvest of the fruits of her labor. Her stories are their stories and their stories are here.

How the holy flaming fuck did I get here? But she knew. It was all about choices. One choice after another choice, and boom, she was a middle-aged married woman with two kids and three dogs in a smelly New York apartment barely big enough for them all.

Oh! And there were wrinkles and gray hairs and a pain in her belly that wouldn't quit. Maybe a hernia, maybe constipation. But try to find a doctor during a plague! Impossible. This was her life now. She was the living, breathing embodiment of a cliche, just with a kinky twist. Gone were her adventures with passionate strangers. Now she dreamed of finding toilet paper at the store. What a fucking world.

Jax cast a cold eye at the ugly weather she saw from the living room window. "Dammit, but oh well," she sighed quietly. Lunch with Carmen couldn't happen. It was pea soup out there. Fog draped the tops of tall buildings under brown and murky skies. The human traffic moved erratically, skidding on ice and jumping over puddles. It annoyed her brain when her plans fell apart. She liked plans. She lived by plans.

A woman fell flat on her face on the sidewalk, startling Jax out of self-pity. Another pedestrian picked up the shoe she lost, put it near her, and kept walking. Everyone else marched blindly past, willing to step over the prone body to stay on schedule.

When people talked about the "energy" of New York City, the fallen woman was its exemplar to Jax. It was a grindingly persistent don't-fuck-with-me energy. Jax went to the coffee machine for a cup of comfort.

No two ways about it, this was starting off as a shitty day. She would survive. She always did. Still, her calendar was almost empty. She hated when there weren't lists and timeslots laid out on her calendar. She had set the day aside for her best friend, and now there was no work she had to do and none she felt like doing. The apartments were all booked, Corey was working in his studio, the kids were taking classes across town and Gigi didn't need her as much now. There was nothing for a Type A personality to do. She paced around the living room, picking up crayons on the sofa and floor and finding a chewed one behind the couch. Was it a child or a dog that reduced it to a pile of chunks?

No one warned her that being a mother was fucking tedious. Just thinking of sweeping out her son's room made her want to slide into a coma. Zane was 12 going on 18. She had already found a couple of stiff, stinky socks under his bed. She had sworn she wouldn't be the kind of mother who'd spy on her kids, but she guiltily got on his computer and found his pubescent porn stash. Lots and lots of anime, endless anime, anime that kind of looked like porn, but she couldn't tell. It wasn't her generation's idea of porn, that was for sure.

And then she found his boob stash. She wasn't disturbed that he had one, but that he was making a determined study of every size, shape, and color of boob in the known universe. He had cataloged and numbered them. What was going on in that pre-man brain of his? What kind of hormonal nightmare was she facing when he hit his teens? Would their place be big enough for a horny teenage boy if another quarantine ever came along?

Being a Femdom and a mother was harder than she ever imagined. The *argue, resist, and conquer* gene had passed directly from mother to son. When she taught her kids to question everything, she had no idea the price she'd have to pay in having Zane constantly question HER. That drove her crazy. Sometimes, she heard her mother Lucille's words coming out of her own mouth and she hated herself for that. She feared his adolescence in a big city. The violence that had erupted throughout the streets of New York could swallow up her only son.

She cleared her mind with deep breaths. She had a child-free afternoon, she reminded herself. A precious few hours of freedom. She usually spent those hours with her best friend, Carmen. They were supposed to meet up at 11 am and have a best-girlfriend day, when they would both feel stupid-young and spend money recklessly. Just two dominant ladies out on the town, shopping for whatever appealed to them and stopping for food they wouldn't keep in their pantries. A large plate of decadent pastry was always involved. Their secret vice.

When Carmen called to postpone, she felt a shadow of depression pass through her. She felt helpless and she hated that feeling.

She flashed back to the fallen woman. It was an omen for sure. Carmen was right. Nothing but hardships and hazards awaited them on the streets. Skidding on frozen sidewalks, leaping over sewer puddles, breaking a heel and landing face-first on the sidewalk. Humiliation and pain lurked ominously on every block. This was no weather for women who liked being in control.

She went to her bed to sit and contemplate her alternatives. She could get lost in yoga. She could work on the kids' home-schooling lessons. Her brain rattled around her skull like a heavy marble. Everything sounded boring. Bills, no. Cleaning, absolutely not. Condo snack inventory... she did it two days ago. That left napping or eating. Or both. Perhaps masturbation, followed by a bath. Or a luxurious bath followed by napsturbation. That actually sounded soothing. She could meditate in the bath, and then napsturbate. That would take her up to dinnertime if she was decadent enough. Maybe bring chocolates and wine to the bath? And her Kindle? Now she had a plan. It didn't include making dinner for four.

"Husband!" she yelled out.

"Whaaat?" Corey yelled back from his studio.

"Make burgers tonight!" she yelled.

"Oooh! Yes, Ma'am!"

She texted him.

Wake me up when you start cooking.

Text?! 😄 😄 U r texting me?
Ur yelling was hot. 💧 💧

Your yelling was not.

Oh. 🙄 Okay. Your wish is my command 👀 😵 😎

That's right.

LOL 😄 😄 🤪 💧

She put the phone down and filled the bath with lavender salts and her favorite bubble bath. She turned the hot water tap open all the way, mesmerized by the water rushing out of the faucet. She pretended it was a mountain creek, splashing and sploshing with furious noise. It would be cool if the pipes occasionally spat out a fish or a little frog. If she lived in the country, she might have a creek, even a small river where she could fish and swim. But she didn't live in the country and even if she did, would she really do any of those things? Besides, that wasn't what she should be thinking about on her one free afternoon in over a month. She needed to focus on things that would make her happy in the here and now.

An emptiness overcame her. Why? Because she was stuck indoors when she should be window shopping with Carmen, trying on outfits they couldn't afford, and devouring puff pastries with abandon while dishing the dirt on their sex lives.

Oh, the horror of it, to be indoors, in a safe apartment with the love of her life. Seriously, what the fuck was wrong with her? Why did she feel so down today? Why couldn't she simply be grateful for all the blessings she had? She had worked her ass off to acquire those blessings. Why couldn't she relax and enjoy them? Instead, she worried about all the "what ifs." What if Zane was growing up too fast, what if Miranda's wild imagination got her in trouble, what if Corey's artistic block never ended, what if, what if? What was the point of what if? What if everything turned out fine, and the kids grew up to be wonderful human beings? She could imagine: Zane becoming a technology wizard, Miranda becoming an artist like her dad, and Corey finally producing the kind of work that got raves from the snotty, snobby, disgusting critics she had come to hate.

She climbed into the claw-footed tub and soaped her heavy round breasts abstractly, waiting to be uplifted by the calming combination of vanilla bubbles and lavender bath salts. She could not be sweetly calmed today with a simple dunk in water. She swished her hips around, but the water felt neutral on her usually sensitive labia. She did breathing exercises, hoping to yoga-away her gray mood. She wanted to feel like a Goddess of Water, but she felt like a big blob of discontented flesh.

She stared down at her naked body, the body Corey always told her was even more beautiful after bearing kids. It wasn't more beautiful to her anymore. There were rolls she could grab with both hands. Everything about her now was bigger and softer. Even her head seemed to have grown. Her jaw was wider, her forehead too, as her hairline had slightly receded with age. Corey said she had curves in all the best places, but she cringed when he told her there was "more to love." Gross. A vague pain in her belly turned sharp, making her catch her breath. The bath had only added to her stress and now her guts were paying the price. Goddammit. The tub was a terrible idea.

She suddenly lunged up and out of the tub with superhuman force, splashing soapy water all over the floor. She threw towels down to soak up the suds and dried off angrily, then stomped off to her bedroom without drying her hair, swigging deeply from the wine bottle. She hesitated at the doorway; she had neatly made the bed. But the hell with neatness! She threw the covers back and curled up on the sheets, put the wine bottle and a box of chocolates on the nightstand, then stared morosely at the penis lamp in the corner of the room. Grandpa Paul made that lamp and just looking at it always made her smile. Not today. Looking at it just made her wish he was still alive. He would know what to do. He would bring her tea and hold her hand and listen to her with an understanding look. She pulled the blanket up to her chin and stuffed two chocolates into her mouth.

She was crying. She was actually crying. She never cried. She blinked away the tears and took another big swig of wine. The tears flowed now. Her guts still ached. She glugged some more wine and felt a little better. She had the wisdom to calm herself, she knew she did. So she got into the Shavasana yoga position, stretching her feet wide apart and placing her arms at her sides, counting her breaths. She wanted to empty her brain of all thought. A spiritual state of nothingness was her goal. Nothing, nothing, nothing, she didn't want to think of anything bad or even good. But suddenly the Corpse Pose spooked her, so she flipped over and reached for more wine. The alcohol was having the desired effect now. Her muscles relaxed, her stomach relaxed, and now all that was left was to relax her overworked brain. She tried another yoga technique, tightening and releasing all the muscle groups in her body, from her toes to her face. It seemed to be working. Her tears dried, her mind began to dissociate, and she could see things more clearly now.

Suddenly, she knew why she was so unhappy. It was the anniversary of Booker's death, she realized grimly. Booker, her first true love and single biggest heartbreak. It was exactly eleven years ago on this day that he committed suicide. She choked back a sob. Would the grieving never end? Or the guilt? She wished she could roll back time. She could have said more or done something different, she could have been there for him in his darkest hour and prevented him from killing himself. Maybe if she'd been a little kinder or listened to him a bit harder, she could have stopped him. She should have stayed in closer touch with him and called him more often. She'd read all the books saying you can't really stop someone from committing suicide, but she clung to the fear that she, she alone, really could have done something if only she'd understood what he was going through.

But nothing could fix it now. And, being honest with herself, she probably couldn't have fixed it then either. By the time she met Corey, her love affair with Booker was ancient history. They'd both moved on to new people, new lives, new obsessions. They had wonderful lives, they'd assured each other during their increasingly infrequent phone calls. Booker stopped confiding in her about his personal life, and she took that as a cue that he didn't want to hear about hers either. They had nothing in common anymore except their failed romance. He couldn't relate to her domesticity, and she couldn't relate to his incessant partying. The last few years of their on-again-off-again conversations were superficial at best.

She tried to forgive herself. Whatever happened, it wasn't her fault. She knew that. She needed to let go of the guilt. It was normal to grieve your first love, especially when they died tragically, inexplicably, and by their own hand. She swigged more wine.

The night before he killed himself, he threw a wild party. He invited her and Corey, who was her fiancé at the time. She remembered being confused by the mix of people who attended the lavish event, replete with waiters in white jackets. He'd invited his father, some friends from his college days, two drag queens, some old boyfriends, and his current mélange of sycophants, gold-diggers, and posers. When she arrived, Booker startled her with a passionate hug. She figured he was high out of his mind and tried to ease out of the hug, but he wouldn't let her go. She remembered the look on Corey's face and silently mouthed, "I'm sorry," to him. He nodded back, and went to get a drink at the bar, where a person in a neon speedo with matching pasties was serving. She followed Corey with her eyes and watched him pretend not to notice that the bartender was trying to flirt with him. She remembered thinking how sweet her man was and how happy she was that they were getting married.

"Attention! Attention!" Booker abruptly called out just at that moment. "Many of you already know her becaaaaause," he slurred, "everyone knows Jax, right? You better know. But for you dummies who don't know Queer history, this is Jax, my perfect, perfect ex-girlfrien'. What a frien' she was. A frien' in need is... what is it? A friend in weed? I should've put a ring on her when we dated."

Jax and Booker's dad exchanged a quick, painful glance. She knew his heart was crying for his boy.

But the crowd roared with laughter, thinking it was hilarious for him to say that. They couldn't imagine their flaming friend being anything other than gay. She blushed deep red. The drugs or whatever he was on made him sloppy, in speech and in body. He leaned against her to steady himself, and she froze, unsure what to do.

Booker laughed with his friends. "I know," he said. "Imagine me married to a girl!" He raised his finger in the air, "Inconthievable!" Again they all laughed.

Did she just imagine the sadness in his eyes, though? After all, he had tried to be straight with her. He hid his gayness from her as long as he could. Who knew what he really thought? She looked for his dad again and saw that he was standing next to Corey at the bar, talking to him. She felt so sorry for the elderly man. He didn't belong in this crowd. Compared to everyone else in the room, her long-haired, bearded, and pierced artist boyfriend looked wholesome. When Booker's dad patted his shoulder, she realized he was congratulating Corey on their engagement. That made her even sadder. She knew he always hoped that she and Booker would somehow reconcile one day.

But Booker charted a new course the minute they broke up and lived his gayness with gusto. He stepped out of the closet with passionate intensity. She thought he was living his best life without her. He had everything to live for -- he was handsome, brilliant, accomplished, and the sole heir to his father's fortune. He had a degree in psychology, he was a trained chef, he even spoke three languages. And he relished all the small pleasures of life, such as acting over the moon happy when he found a new cheese at Zabar's or stopping to pet every dog he saw. He made it a hobby to cook fabulous meals for good looking but down-on-their-luck men, saying it was one way he could pay back his Community for all the fun he had. His kitchen became a restaurant that served only one horny customer at a time, which they both found amusing at the time. Of course, a lot of the men who ate his Seared Scallops and Kobe Beef were rent-boys and one-night stands, but there was one guy he invited to move in. She couldn't remember the guy's name, but she remembered that guy clearly because Booker once hired her to rescue him from a BDSM club when she was working as a cabbie. She'd never forget that strange night, nor the awkwardly uncomfortable conversation they had that night.

First, he bribed her with a ridiculous sum to go fetch his boyfriend, then he insisted that she needed to move in with them and become the guy's Mistress so they could all live happily ever after. She briefly considered it out of her love for him, but by the time she got home that night she was pissed off. Booker treated her like a commodity, not a friend, like the Pro-Domme, Mistress Amazon, she once was, rather than the girl named Jax who he once loved. That was the beginning of the end between them. She took off for Massachusetts with Paul the very next day and avoided Booker's calls for a year after that.

She regretted describing Booker to Corey as a fucked-up liar who thought she would save him from being gay until she finally realized that all the nights Booker said he couldn't see her because he was studying were nights he spent in the arms of men. She felt ashamed of herself now for diminishing their relationship and what it meant to her at the time. It was wrong. He was a good person. Even if he lied to her. He never meant to hurt her. She was sure of that much.

She couldn't remember the name of the guy he wanted her to dominate, but it started with a D. What was his name? Dick? Dirk? Dan? Doofus! That's how she remembered him: he was a total doofus. A tall blonde from some Midwestern hick town, awkward in speech and clumsy as fuck. When she studied him in the rearview mirror that night, she was flummoxed. What could that bland man have in common with the elegant, sophisticated, graceful Booker, the perfectly groomed scion of African-American royalty? In retrospect, considering the kind of men who skittered through Booker's life later on, maybe Doofus wasn't the worst choice. Certainly not as bad as the airheads shoveling coke up their noses at the last party. She didn't see Doofus at the party. She wondered why.

Corey appeared at the bedroom door. She looked at him morosely and took another gulp of wine. "What?" she asked dully.

"Um. Was it something I didn't say?"

"What? What do you mean?"

"You're drinking early," he said.

"I'm drinking on my own schedule today. Leave me alone."

"I see. Well, sorry to bother you, Madame, but did you see my harness? I remember taking it off on the couch last night, but it isn't there."

"You left a leather harness on the couch! Where the kids could find it?"

"I wasn't thinking, I was too tired."

"I'll bet it's in Zane's room! Holy crap, Corey. Shit."

She leaped out of bed and they ran down the hall together to Zane's room.

"Bonus," Corey said, reaching to touch her naked ass.

"STOP NOW," she barked. "This isn't the time."

He meekly took his hand back. "Jeez, honey," he muttered.

She threw open the door to her son's bedroom and scanned it intently. Sure enough, black leather straps were piled next to Zane's gaming set-up. "Oh, man," she said, then grabbed them in her hand. "That child is going to give me a nervous breakdown."

"What did he do to them?" Corey inspected the disassembled harness, bemused. The leather straps had been neatly cut off, leaving only stray rivets still embedded in discarded scraps. "He destroyed it," he concluded.

"Thank you, Captain Obvious. Now we have to explain why we have a leather harness in the house. Not to mention the cost of replacing the harness. Goddammit, Corey, this is the dumbest thing you've ever done."

"Oh, surely I've done dumber things."

"Not now," she growled. "This isn't funny."

Corey paused. "He probably doesn't know what it is," he tried to reassure her.

"He's in puberty, for God's sake. He knows what it is."

"At his age, I was more interested in action figures," Corey said. "Maybe he's building an action figure or something."

"Did I not tell you about his stiff socks?"

"Oh yeah," he chuckled. "Right. He's in puberty! Still, he's only 12. Let's pretend we got it for the dog."

"The dog?! Which one could wear a leather harness that size?? The Chihuahua or the two Jack Russells?"

"Let's buy a Great Dane! We'll surprise him when he gets home!"

Jax frowned. "I guess we can say you got it for an art project."

"I guess that's easier."

"Though, now that you mention it, I wouldn't mind getting a big dog for protection, if you were serious about that. Maybe a German Shepherd or a Rottweiler."

"Because there aren't enough furniture-chewing, carpet-destroying, indoor shitters around here?"

"Don't talk like that about our fur babies!"

"And yet, it's undeniably true. They are literally home-wreckers."

She glared at him, then turned her back on him and stormed off to the kitchen. He followed her in silence.

She searched the wine cabinet. "We can't be out of Cabernet."

"I'll make you some coffee," he said.

"I don't need more coffee. I need anti-coffee. I need more wine."

"You took the last bottle."

"Fuck no. Are you kidding me? Well, crap." She sank into a chair and put her head on the table.

"You doing okay?"

"Do I look like I'm doing okay?" she asked without lifting her head. "I'm trying to force myself to have a whole day of relaxation."

"That sounds very stressful."

"You have no idea!"

He fixed coffee for himself and squeezed a lemon into sparkling water for her.

"Here, have some Vitamin C."

"Thanks." She swallowed the sour water and wrinkled her nose. "Tastes like foamy piss."

"Honey." He put his hand over hers sympathetically. "What's going on? I've never seen you this down."

"Well, you know how I never usually worry about Marco, but one of his boys tested positive for COVID two days ago." She paused. "Of course, he's fully vaxxed. He'll probably be okay."

"Okay then. He'll be fine, I'm sure. Plus there's Paxlovid now. You can stop worrying."

She let out a sob, then another followed and she covered her face with her hands. She couldn't hold it back now.

"Sweetheart, what's the matter? Jax, honey." He put his arms around her and hugged her hard. "What's wrong, did something happen? Is it Gigi?"

"It's eleven years since Booker killed himself. It's the anniversary."

"Oh, Jax, I'm so sorry. Wow. Eleven years. Well." His eyes grew soft and tender. "I didn't realize you kept track of the anniversary."

"I remember all of them. My father's. Steve's. Booker's. David's. Paul's. Bingo's."

"You remember the anniversary of Bingo's death?"

"Yes, of course, I do."

"Bingo was a dog."

"So what?" she said. "He was a person to me."

"That's so Goth!!" he deflected. "It's kind of hot, actually."

Jax humphed and turned to stare out the kitchen window.

He followed her gaze. "I see the sun is trying to break through. Might be good to take a walk and breathe some fresh air."

"Fresh air in this city? What's next, fresh water from the East River?"

"Wow," he said. "I'm starting to worry about you. Maybe lay off the wine, eh?"

"I'm going to walk the dogs and come back with more wine," she said. "Now I'm pissed we let the weather cancel our plans. Dammit. I'd be eating pastries with Carmen right now. I can't believe the sun is shining NOW, when it should've been shining this morning. Fucking meteorologists!"

"Aww, it sucks having so much power and privilege that you resent the weather." Corey wiggled his eyebrows at her.

Finally, she laughed. He leaned over her and she leaned into him, letting him hug her and nestle his face in her neck, lingering in the moment, inhaling the comforting smell of his familiar body. He always smelled so good to her, a sweet woody smell of pine and oak that relaxed her.

"You're right, I'm a privileged bitch and I need to quit pitying myself."

"You said it!" Corey smiled and kissed her on the head. "Go out, you'll feel better. Have a nice long walk with your four-legged children. Buy yourself something special."

"I've had my eye on a bottle of Mark Ryan's Water Witch at the wine store for weeks now."

Corey opened his lips and then closed them diplomatically. "Whatever you wish, Mistress."

As he left the room, she stared at his fine ass. That man was fine all over. Yeah, she was lucky. He was a good guy. She loved him and the kids to her core, so much it almost hurt, but in a good way. She was the luckiest.

Today. Here and now. That was what mattered. Not the past. Not the unknowable future. That's what Grandpa Paul always said. "Live in the here and now."

As she dressed, she repeated those words. Today she had a beautiful family. Corey was an angel. Their kids were adorable little people. The dogs made her laugh every day. They had money in the bank. She was living a good, solid, normal life. Like a normal American. Plus, she was the head of a large, loving Leather Family. She had every reason to be happy.

Beams of sunlight poured through the bedroom window, lighting up the floor and walls and drying the damp sheets with their warmth. She would be alright. Everything would be okay. She was okay.

She pulled on tight black jeans, one of Corey's blue work shirts, and shiny black rubber boots so she could slosh through mud puddles with the dogs. She topped off the black and blue ensemble with a small ruby heart that Corey gave her for her last birthday. She admired herself in the mirror. She was practically a walking Leather Flag. Nobody would know that except for people like her, and that was OK. In her book, everyone in the lifestyle was her kin.

The dogs were sleeping in their own tiny room, once a servant's quarters, and hardly bigger than a closet. She never understood how a human could stand to sleep in that space, but their tiny dogs had room to zoom and play. Three small cozy beds were arranged for them there, and she added dog bone-printed curtains and bowls for them. But really, the decor was for her because their aesthetics were non-existent. She smiled at that. It was a good sign that she was cracking herself up again.

She gently pushed open the door to find them already waggling their tails furiously.

"Who wants park walkies? Who wants to go to the park?"

With a chorus of woofs and whines, they scrambled to their feet and danced around her legs. She crouched down to snuggle with them.

"Hello good boys, hello good girl, hello, hello, my darlings, hello Pandora, yes, you may kiss me, hello Chico, and hello The Man, wait for Pandora to finish, okay, there we go." One by one the boys got on their backs for tummy rubs, while Pandora, the contagiously jolly chihuahua, tongue-cleaned Jax's nostrils with undying love.

"Aghhh!" she laughed, pushing Pandora off. "Agggh, don't eat my nose, Pandora! Not the Mistressly nose!"

When she opened the door they exploded into the hallway and raced to the front door, squirming with excitement. She should have played with them instead of trying to take a bath. They were instant mood-lifters in all their goofy, over-the-top joy.

"Sit!" she commanded, folding her arms. Chico was so excited he could barely make his behind stop wiggling enough to make contact with the floor.

"Good babies," she said, then attached their leashes. Cooing over them, she continued, "Such good doggies, yes you are." They panted with happiness. "Ok, kids, let's go!"

Off they went, out the door and down to the street, the middle-aged mommy and her pack of yippy pups, merging into the sidewalk traffic.

"Are you happy, my babies? Mommy is happy to be with you!" she sang to them. Pandora looked over her tiny shoulder and flashed a sweet doggy smile as if she understood English.

"That's right, baby girl," Jax said. "Shopping and pastries was so this-morning," she continued. "We're going to kick up some mud in the park and reclaim the day."

The word park electrified the dogs, who began tugging at their leashes.

When they reached the corner of Central Park West, the dogs raised their muzzles, noses twitching wildly, sucking up the smells that awaited them on the other side. They body-bumped each other's flanks with excitement.

Yes. Here and now life was good. Everything was good. Jax waved her free arm. "I AM HAPPY, NEW YORK!" she shouted to no one.

"Lady, nobody fuckin' cares," a stranger spat out as he walked around them and crossed the avenue ahead of them.

"Goddamn New Yorkers," she muttered under her breath, wishing she'd brought an umbrella to poke the bastard. "That's the problem with New York. It's infested with New Yorkers."

The second they got inside the park, the dogs became different animals. Busy sniffing everything, pulling her to every spot they could smell urine so they could pee over on top of it, occasionally lingering over a pile of poop as if trying to figure out which dogs had better diets.

"Leave that shit alone," she called out to the boys who looked ready to taste it and evaluate whether there was a dog in the neighborhood who ate better than them. She pulled them away. "No shitty snouts today," she announced. "Nope, not cleaning that up, not today, my fine hounds."

If only they could have their own backyard instead of a dirty public park filled with God only knew how many diseases and toxins. They said dogs could catch COVID. What if...?

No. She wouldn't allow herself to wonder "what if." There was a better future for her family and, she swore to herself, it would not be in New York.

ℬ Chapter 2 ℭ

WE'RE ONLY OLD ONCE

You can be old in numbers yet as young as playful kids at heart. Your body may show the scars and wrinkles of time but your spirit can remain forever adventurous. Life is not linear in the end, it advances in infinity loops, moving forward and backward and side to side as long as you learn to adapt to change and grow your mind.

On a sunny street in the middle of the world, where birds sang and flowers bloomed, heavy doors concealed the secrets behind them, just as they do all around the world. So if you peeked through a small window on the door of house number 2024, you'd see a spacious foyer. A table with a crystal vase on the right. A carpeted staircase on the left. Nothing unusual to be gleaned here because these residents hid their true lives from the world behind curtains and partitions and a few sound-insulated walls. Their true lives were kinky lives, and as their resident Matriarch declared, "Ain't nobody's business what we do in here."

This particular day would be memorable, though it started as it had always started for 43 years. Gigi, the Matriarch, woke first, donned her standard morning attire of black leather slippers and a black satin robe, passing by the small window next to the front door, and, by habit, peered outside. She didn't like visitors and had a small plaque saying "No Solicitors" to ward off Mormons, Jehovah's Witnesses, and other door-to-door salespeople peddling their brand and wasting her time. She had moved here for peace, quiet, and privacy above all. After decades on the road, sometimes living in pensions and private homes, she relished having a permanent and somewhat impenetrable home of their own.

Her slavegirl Mili proposed getting a sign that said "beware of venomous snakes" but Gigi thought that might only draw more attention to the house, or worse, encourage snake enthusiasts to drop by.

"Snake enthusiasts?!" Mili exploded with laughter. "Ma'am, what??"

"Imagine if someone who enjoys the company of copperheads wanted to visit," slave Leon said drily.

"Imagine how rattled rattlesnake lovers would be if they stepped into our dungeon," Milli volleyed. "They'd slither right out."

"They're all snakes in the grass," Leon said.

Gigi stuck with her no soliciting plaque and thus far it seemed to work. She sighed happily, turned on the coffee maker, and inspected her mugs. "She Who Must Be Obeyed" was her favorite, but today she went with "Queen of Everything."

Two old German Shepherds, Taco and Django, wandered in and immediately collapsed on the floor to nap. "Hello, boys," Gigi acknowledged them, "I see that sleeping all night tired you out."

She sipped slowly, reviewing her email and scrutinizing her "to-do" list on her phone. She planned every hour of the day, for herself and her slaves. There were chores to be done. There were projects to complete and laundry to wash. There were meals to be had and, after dinner, she let her health decide whether they'd relax or play or both.

Some days she added specific scenes to the calendar. "Wednesday, 4 pm, tell Milli to wear her tutu" or "Monday, 9 am, make Leon clean the bathrooms with a toothbrush (he can wear rubber gloves this time)." She did that to keep the power flowing. Being in charge was not a burden to her, it was a lively game.

Leon popped his head through the doorway.

"May I come in?"

"Do you deserve to come in?" She kept clicking on her phone.

"I hope so, Ma'am, I've been good. I fixed the doorknob on my room so it's easy to get in."

"Ahh, good boy." She put her phone down and opened her arms. "Come give Mistress a hug, then make your coffee and make me a second cup."

He scurried over to hold her gently, then took her mug, faking shock that it wasn't the one she used most days.

"Oooh, you're stretching your own boundaries and switching things up today."

"Shut your mug," she said, biting back a smile.

"My cup is full, Ma'am." He bowed his head.

"You'll be weeding today," she said, "it's getting overgrown."

"Lucky me."

"Want to try that again?"

"Thank you for the privilege of weeding your pot plants, Mistress."

Milli appeared. "May I come in?"

"Good morning, Milli, line up, Leon will make your coffee, too, today."

"Thank you, Ma'am," they both chimed.

Gigi casually inspected their naked bodies, then stared at their feet.

"How are those bunny slippers?"

"Oh, good, good," Leon said. "I'm getting used to them."

"They're too flat for me," Milli said, "my arches hurt."

"Well, we certainly would not want you to suffer to please me!"

"Yes, Ma'am. I mean, no Ma'am, I am happy to suffer for you, Ma'am."

"You have permission to buy a new pair on Amazon. Only one condition: they have to look as ridiculous as those rabbits."

"I already saw some cute raccoon slippers with more of a heel."

"You hear that, Leon? She already saw raccoon slippers. Milli, you can put on your orthotic shoes today, but I expect to see the sweat dripping down the crack of your ass because you're working so hard on the kitchen curtains! I will be inspecting your work."

Milli curtseyed. "Yes, Ma'am, thank you, Ma'am."

"Leon, your weeding today will be supervised. You've neglected the weeds. No one likes messy weeds, least of all weed."

"No, Ma'am, no weeds in the weed, I am on it."

"Any messy weeds I find will be wet with your tears!"

"I understand, Ma'am, I understand."

"Let's do morning affirmations, then we can have breakfast." Her slaves quickly sat down at the table with her and joined hands.

"We believe in ourselves," she said.

"We believe in ourselves," they echoed.

"We are here by choice."

"We are here by choice."

"We belong to Mistress Gigi by choice."

"We belong to Mistress Gigi by choice." Leon bowed his head.

"We have free will and this is the life we choose."

"We have free will and this is the life we choose."

"We are happy in this life." They repeated it, then Gigi paused meaningfully.

"I am happy in this life."

She looked at Milli. Her girl always teared up at this part. "I am happy in this life," Milli said, eyes shimmering. She mouthed, "I love you." Gigi smiled.

She turned to Leon. "I am SO happy in this life, Ma'am, I've never been this happy. Thank you, Lucinda, so much, for all you do for us." He got down on the floor and kneeled before her.

Gigi cleared her throat sternly.

"I mean Mistress Gigi!" Leon added. "My apologies, Ma'am."

She stood up from the table, then leaned down over him. "Do you need help getting up?"

"No, no, I'm fine," he forced himself up, his knees popping like a transmitter about to blow. "See? I'm fine."

"Good enough." She opened her arms again and they had a group hug.

"I love you both dearly and will be checking in with you about two hours from now."

Exactly 2 hours later, on the nose, Gigi strode into the greenhouse in her daywear: black jeans, black boots and a pale blue tunic with a low neck that showed the tops of her boobs. There was an informal agreement among the Doms in Leather Family that they would wear black or blue garments as often as possible. Gigi suggested it as a kind of uniform that would define their place in their families. She loved clothing rituals and the others -- Jax, Carmen, Marco, and Mariangela loved the idea.

She walked proudly toward the greenhouse. Her figure was remarkably good for her age and she liked to show it off. She pulled her white hair into a high ponytail, adding flashy earrings that sparkled with every step. She was feeling better than she had in weeks, so much better that she put on some make-up to feel even better. She used concealer to hide her age-spots, an eyebrow pencil to add drama to her brows, a touch of mascara to make her lashes visible once more, and red lipstick that matched the leather crop hanging off her belt. She looked beautiful to herself in the mirror. If her slaves didn't notice, she would give them hell.

"How are the weeds coming along?"

Leon looked up and then quickly stood at attention. He was naked except for gloves and a harvesting pouch.

"Hello, Mistress! Wow! You look gorgeous today."

"Thank you, slave."

"Got a few ready for harvest!" He shook the canvas bag tied around his waist.

She stuck her right hand in the bag, counting up the buds he'd reaped. Then she grabbed his balls with her left hand. "Are you sure this is everything?" she asked.

"Yes, Mistress, that's everything."

"Are you sure?" She reached around and spread his ass cheeks with her fingers. "You're not hiding anything in there, are you?"

Leon's face bloomed pink. He grinned in embarrassment. "No, Ma'am, no hiding."

Gigi took his penis in hand, then squeezed it until Leon squealed. Her hands ached, but her grip was as fierce as a steel clamp.

"ARE YOU SURE?" She intensified her grip and he bobbed up on his toes, grimacing from the pain.

"Sure, sure," he panted, "very sure!"

She knew better. He loved playing this game with her on harvesting days, hiding a sticky bud in creative places. In an armpit, under his balls, once inside his mouth. It was a little game they liked to play. So she squeezed him until he threw his head back and groaned. A bud fell to the ground. It had been hidden between his clenched ass cheeks.

"Your ass is grass! Seriously, Leon? Now Milli's going to bake your ass grass in brownies and we'll be eating your ass?? That's disgusting."

"Jeez, how did that get there?" Leon protested. "It must have fallen in there when I wasn't looking!"

"And your ass cheeks just grabbed it?"

"I, I don't know, they must have, I guess."

"Prehensile ass cheeks, that's a new one," she laughed. "I think you want an ass whipping."

With that, she grabbed her pliable partner and pulled him close. She flicked her crop on his ass a few times to warm him up, then began to whip him steadily as a metronome. Scarlet streaks blossomed on his cheeks. He begged and pleaded for her to stop. But she knew he didn't want her to stop. He wanted every last painful blow she landed on his ass.

Milli must have heard his screams because she appeared in the greenhouse doorway, panting from her sprint.

"Do you need help, Ma'am? Is the slave boy being bad again? I brought a paddle!"

Leon sighed. "You bitch!"

"Did you hear that, Milli? He called you a bitch. What are you going to do about it?"

In seconds, Milli brought a chair to Gigi. "Please make yourself comfortable, Ma'am. I'll take care of this!"

Gigi sat down. Milli was a saint. She knew it was getting harder for Gigi to use a heavy paddle, what with her arthritis. Even whips and crops were getting hard to flip around the way she did when she was in her 40s. Her body was paying the price of her busy youth. Her right shoulder needed a replacement from all the whip throwing. Her spine was a mess from wearing spiked heels.

Milli led Leon to the steel drum they'd put on its side and secured to the floor for such occasions. Leon bent over it, grunting until his ass was vulnerable and exposed.

"May I, Ma'am?"

"Of course, sweetheart. Give it your best!"

Leon shuddered in anticipation.

Then WHOMP, the first cruel thud of the paddle landed so hard that Leon shrieked.

"My God, Leon, we have neighbors, slut!" Gigi scolded Leon. "Millie, get him a gag."

Gigi checked her watch. "Never mind. We're running late as it is. Give me your panties!"

Milli lifted her skirt and hurried out of her lacy panties.

"These are wet!" She shook her head at Milli. "Did I order you to get excited?"

No matter how many times Gigi said that phrase in their years together, Milli's face always turned bright red. "No, Ma'am."

"Stuff them into the slave boy's mouth," Gigi said. "Make sure the crotch goes in first so he can taste you."

Milli blushed and did as told. Now Leon was wriggling with excitement.

"Milli, continue the paddling. Make sure he KNOWS he was a bad, bad boy again."

Milli danced around with the paddle, eyes glinting. On the one hand, she wanted to do a good job. On the other hand, she knew if she didn't do a really good job, she would be the next one to be spanked. She settled on giving him a few horrific spanks, but easing up on other ones and pretending to miss a few.

"Well, oh my god, you are just two little piggies. Two piggies in a pod. Now tell me, Leon, what is your analysis of Milli's performance?"

"It hurt like hell!" The panties fell out of his mouth as he yelled the words.

"But some of those strokes were weak, weren't they, Leon?"

"I don't want to get Milli in trouble," he said.

"She's already in trouble," Gigi said. "Go ahead."

"Well, yeah, it could have been harder overall," Leon said calmly. "She definitely gave me some baby strokes."

"Milli!"

"Yes, Ma'am?"

"You know you deserve to be spanked for that ridiculous performance, right?"

She feigned shock. "Me, Ma'am?!"

"I think you deliberately slowed down so you could get a spanking."

"Oh nooo, Ma'am, I would never, I just got tired." Milli was playing coy, hoping she would get a better spanking than the one she had given Leon.

Gigi just smiled and stood up.

"Milli, do you know how to punish a masochist?"

Milli giggled and nodded enthusiastically -- then saw the look in Gigi's eyes and paused. "Maybe?"

"You don't give them what they want." Gigi stood up. "Put the chair back and take the paddle back into the house and put it in the dungeon. On the bed. For tonight. When I give you the paddling you really deserve."

Milli gulped. Leon gulped with her. They knew what that meant. Getting their just desserts at the end of the day meant that Milli was getting a seriously, excruciatingly painful spanking tonight. They held their breath, tantalized by the threat.

"I love you, Ma'am," Milli blurted.

"As it should be, girl," Gigi said, walking away and leaving the greenhouse to let them stew in their own kinky juices.

* * *

They had traveled long and they had traveled well. They'd unpacked their bags in Lisbon and Dubai, Mallorca, Hong Kong, and on the Riviera. They'd shopped in Paris and London. They had seen the world without ever once leaving their happy bubble of triadic inner peace, the peace that grew with every year and aged like fine wine. The sharp edges were gone. They had ripened and evolved together until there was nothing but the happy bubble, a mystically whole shield that guaranteed them safe passage wherever they went.

And then came the pandemic. The decision was swift. They would go home. The United States called to them now. They urgently wanted to be back in their native land, close to their family. Not that they could do much for others, but they wanted to wait out the plague with their own kind. It was time.

A few phone calls to Jax later, they flew to New York that March and moved into a small condo Jax owned. But after a year of living in New York, they decided they needed to flee. It was too congested, too complicated, and too stressful. They wanted space to spread out, perhaps a real home after decades of small hotels and cramped boarding houses. New York was not for old people. The sidewalks were terrifying in winter and the apartment felt suffocating in the summer. With the Lock Down, they felt suffocated in the tiny apartment Jax let them stay in for free. She was losing money because of them. They couldn't take advantage of her kindness forever.

Jax stepped in once more to help. She recognized they needed to relocate to a calmer, quieter place. She agreed with them that the city was in chaos. She called Marco in Denver to see if they could do better out there. In two weeks, he found them a fire sale on the perfect house. It was in a beautiful 1950s subdivision with big homes, wide lawns, and quiet streets. It sat on 2 acres and was surrounded by spruce, fir, and pine. The previous owners died suddenly of COVID and their heirs were desperate to sell. The price had been slashed and the house would go into bankruptcy if they didn't close a deal soon.

"Why is it selling so cheap?" Jax asked. "The price is crazy low."

"The backyard," Marco explained. "They were farmers or something. One look at the backyard and the buyers left. You couldn't just mow it down and it had an old irrigation system that was busted. Plus a dilapidated greenhouse. It could work for them."

Finally, Jax had good news for Gigi. Marco found a move-in ready house for them in a tranquil suburb of Denver. The elders, long accustomed to adapting to settling into whatever setting Karma brought their way, were charmed by this vision of all-American life in suburbia. They oohed and aahed and squeezed each other's hands when they visited for the first time. There were five bedrooms, a large living room, a huge kitchen, and three bathrooms. Such luxury after years of living in cramped spaces! They all agreed their favorite part was a cinder-block-lined basement. It seemed perfect for a dedicated dungeon, a luxury they hadn't known since they left the US. There was even an extra bedroom down there.

The greenhouse made them laugh and wink knowingly at each other. It needed updating, but the house was solidly built. The front lawn was perfectly manicured. Only the neglected garden would be costly to renovate. It was a jungle of scrub and thorny vines. Gigi didn't care. They were not outdoorsy. They were sit-on-a-patio-and-drinksy. The old greenhouse charmed her and was perfect to grow pot now that weed was legal in Colorado. It would save them a lot of money. Between the greenhouse and the huge back patio with a built-in barbecue, they had all the outdoor space they needed.

The day they arrived in Colorado, one of Marco's boys stood waiting for them with a sign that said, "Jax's Family." And, in fact, Jax was with them. She had offered to travel with them and help them get organized for a couple of weeks. Marco's boy, Wesley, a shy, handsome man in his 30s, waved to them and quickly arranged their luggage on a cart. He led them to a shiny SUV in the parking lot, loaded the baggage while they climbed inside the vehicle, and off they went.

"Wesley," Jax said, "I'm glad to meet you! Marco's told me a lot about you, but how about you tell me something about yourself." She sat in the front seat with Google Maps open while the elders crowded into the back. They bounced excitedly, pointing out the window. "Did you see that?" "Oh, what the hell is that?"

Wesley was distracted by their chatter, but finally answered Jax. "I'm a graphic artist?"

"Aren't you sure?" Milli piped up.

"What? I'm a graphic artist? Have you seen my Insta yet?"

"Insta what?" Gigi asked. "Is that some kind of electric car?"

Wesley got tight-lipped and looked straight ahead.

"They're older than us," Jax lowered her voice, "and they've been away a long time."

"Oh, that's okay," Wesley shrugged, "my grandparents don't know Insta either."

"That's probably for the best, right?"

"Totes," he said.

"I had a Totes once," Milli interjected, "but it broke during a storm in Milan."

"Not that kind of Totes, darling," Jax said. Confused whispers ensued in the back seat.

Wesley got off the highway, took a few turns and they finally pulled up to the house. Leon was the first one out of the car. He paced around, inhaling. "I love this air!" He pounded his chest. "I haven't smelled air like this since we were in Slovenia."

Gigi opened the door and her slaves darted excitedly into the house. Wesley didn't seem to know what to do. He finally came to the doorway and dropped to his knees, anxiously checking his phone and waiting for Marco (or maybe God) to tell him what to do next. Gigi could not believe her eyes.

"Git!" she ordered him. "Get inside, git! I don't need the neighbors to see you kneeling! Jesus fucking Christ, kid. This isn't the Castro."

Wesley was discombobulated. "Sorry, Ma'am, sorry! I was waiting for orders?"

Gigi snorted impatiently and showed him into the kitchen. "Make yourself useful. See if you can find coffee and make some for everyone."

"Yes, Ma'am. Ma'am?"

"Now what?"

"What if I can't find coffee?"

"See the coffee machine? Do you know how to work that coffee machine?"

He peered. "Yes, Ma'am. My gran had one just like that."

"Good, then if you can't find coffee, go to a store and buy whatever coffee the machine takes and bring it home."

Wesley brightened up. "Yes, Ma'am! I'm on it!"

The group went exploring the house room by room. As befit her rank, Gigi chose first. The master suite on the upper level was exactly what she'd hoped it would be: big, but not too big, with original moldings and architectural details around the gracious bay window overlooking the garden. The queen-size bed had a beautifully carved headboard, matching end tables and a magnificent dresser with a large, ornate mirror.

Jax walked in and turned green. It was opulently tacky, faux French provincial everything, even the lamps, and the most hideous carpeting she'd ever seen.

"I love this!" Gigi cried. "I just love the shag rug! I haven't seen one since the 1970s! My rich Aunt Nelly had furniture like this. She promised me I'd inherit the whole set!" Gigi's face fell at the memory. "Then she took me out of her will like I didn't exist."

Jax squeezed her arm. The old lady leaned on her for a moment.

"Ah, well, fuck Aunt Nelly. Now I've got an even better set."

Jax kissed her cheek. "You deserve a better set than she had!"

"I do," Gigi said. "I was her favorite niece. Until she found out what I did for a living."

Jax touched her friend's arm and Gigi shrugged. "Whaddya gonna do about people like that?"

"Ignore them. And get better furniture."

"Exactly! You read my mind."

They went back into the hall where Milli was inspecting a small room close to the master suite, probably built as a nursery, with only a tiny closet and space enough for a twin bed and small dresser.

"Isn't it a little claustrophobic?" Gigi asked.

"Yeah! Like a prison cell!" Milli said. "I want it. Besides, it's closest to your room."

"We'll hear each other's farts and snores," Gigi said.

"Yeah," Milli glowed. "It'll be cozy and romantic."

"Oh my God," Jax interjected, "what are you even talking about?"

Milli and Gigi cracked up. "It's called the reality of life," Gigi said.

"Fuck reality," Jax said, "this is your dream home! We'll insulate the walls. Maybe install air filters." They laughed.

Leon took the room at the other end of the hall, where a Superman blanket covered a twin bed. Star Wars figures, Transformers, and G.I. Joes lined the shelves.

"Ideal!" Leon said. He plopped on top of Superman. "I'm going to need a better mattress."

They went to another room. It had an unusually large window. Gigi shut the door when she spotted a folded wheelchair, a bedpan, boxes of gauze and other medical supplies. Linoleum lined the floor. "Forget we saw that."

"Wait, that's a handy room!" Leon said.

"Shut up," Gigi said.

"What? I meant for medical play."

"Jax, come here!" Gigi beckoned her to the last room on that floor. It was nicely appointed, but utterly monotone.

"It's all beige!" Milli said. "So beige."

"Going for the hotel look," Jax said as she went inside. "Probably their guest room. Good size too."

"Think you could make it more colorful?" Gigi asked Jax.

"Of course! Would you like me to redo it for you? As a housewarming present?"

"No, I'd like you to redo it for yourself."

"What do you mean?"

"I want this bedroom to be yours. This is where you will stay when you visit. You can fix it up however you like so it feels like a second home when you stay here."

Milli clapped her hands. "Yes! Jax's room!"

"Oh my god, you guys. Don't you need the room?"

"Milli put an arm around Jax's waist. "We love you so much."

"You've done so much for us, Jax," Leon said as he put his arms around them both. "You rescued us."

And so the Family elders found their first and last house. This is where they would peacefully live and peacefully die one day and that thought gave them comfort. They would be together until the bitter end, taking care of each other, helping each other to live and die with dignity. There would be no more voyages filled with uncertainty and anxiety, no more struggling to lead a normal life, no more temporary residences, no more instability. The feelings they felt that first day never went away. They had found their one true permanent home.

* * *

"I'm too tired to paddle tonight," Gigi said.

"Aw, that's okay, Ma'am," Milli said. Milli was sitting on the bed with her, reading the Internet. She loved to lurk on a local gossip board. It kept them up-to-date on everything from local emergencies to sales at the grocery stores. She also found a thread discussing who had bought up their home, which the neighbors called "the old Gordon place." Some said they were a wife, husband, and mother-in-law. Others said they had proof they were two sisters and a brother. Milli read the latest installment. "Ooh! Listen to this! Now, we're some kind of operatives secretly working for Q. We're part of the plan!"

"What plan?

"Nobody knows. It's just a plan."

"What the hell does that mean?" Gigi was irritated.

Leon walked in. "Everything okay? I thought there would be screams by now."

"Mistress is too tired to play."

"No problem, no problem," Leon said. "Is there anything I can do for you, Gigi?"

"Leon!" Milli exclaimed. "Guess what?! According to Harriet Hornwhistle on Blossom Way, you're my older brother who I'm protecting from the law and Gigi is our aunt!"

"Are those fucking idiots still at it?" Leon howled. "What is wrong with these people? Don't they have better things to do with their lives?"

"Ma'am, are you my auntie now?"

"All I know is I'm a fuck of a long way from Lucinda's world," Gigi sighed. "I want to go back in the time machine."

"Awwwww, Mistress, don't say that! You don't. This is the best place we've ever lived."

Gigi closed her eyes and lay flat on her pillow. "The people around here, Jesus Fucking Christ. The old ones were the worst, too!" Had she really grown up with those pricks? And now she was among them. Had she made the right choice coming here? Her fingers shot to her temples as if massaging them could make the serotonin flow.

"Let me do that for you, please, Mistress?" Milli scooted over and Gigi relaxed against her.

Leon curled up at her feet. "Let me relax you." He gently massaged her feet. A wave of relaxation swept over her as the familiar hands rubbed away her foot aches. Milli massaged her arms and shoulders, gently stretching her joints.

Gigi gave herself to the four loving hands on her body the way her slaves gave themselves to her whip. With vulnerability. With trust.

"You are my life," she finally murmured. "You may go now. I love you." She heard them tiptoe out of the room and Gigi rolled over to hug her pillow.

They had traveled the world together. They'd seen everything they wanted to see together. The days of being Mistress Lucinda were a nanosecond in a much larger life, the life of adventure with her two wonderful partners. What more could anyone want out of life?

Was she happy? She didn't know. What was it like to be happy -- was it like this? She was happier now than she had been when they traveled. Happier than she ever remembered. She wasn't happy as a child or a teen. Mistress Lucinda was too paranoid about betrayals to feel entirely happy, though she knew she reached her highest peaks of pleasure when she was alone with her slaves. She remembered the hundreds of virile suitors who once pleaded to serve. The things they did. What a life! But that was long ago, far away, yesterday. Today they'd walk with canes if they still walked at all.

It all seemed like a dream to her now, the years she spent living dangerously, the time when she seduced every man she wanted and showed off her body with delight. Who could desire her today? She was the same woman, the same Goddess! She simply inhabited a different body now.

She inhaled and exhaled and inhaled and exhaled until her heartbeat slowed.

She counted her blessings. Yes, blessed she was. She'd won. She'd outlived the hunters, the hurters, the haters. She'd won.

She remembered what she said to Leon when his knee failed him during a tour of Angkor Wat and he couldn't walk for a while.

"It's over for me," he said, crying. "I'm done. You're only young once."

"You're only old once, too and you are NOT done," Gigi said. "We'll find a doctor to fix the leg and you'll be your annoying old self in no time." Her tone made him stand back up and limp to the bus with them. And sure enough, it was just a strained ligament, something that had happened once before, ironically when he was young.

They managed it. They managed everything together. They were a holy trinity of true grit. The truest grit. And they felt the comfort of the Leather Family they had joined. God bless Jax, Jax who met them by chance in Europe and carried her love for them back across the ocean. Jax joined their triad to Marco's triad and Carmen's couple during a series of epic virtual meetings on the Internet. A year later, Jax and Corey, Carmen and Lo, and Marco and his boys met in Montreux for the jazz festival and the die was cast. They dedicated themselves to the others and the others welcomed them in as cherished elders.

At first, Gigi saw herself -- a younger, sweeter self -- in Jax. It was like a dream come true, as if a daughter she didn't know she had was waiting for her all along. These days, she felt more like Jax's daughter than her mother because Jax had so many more responsibilities in her life, while Gigi was a lady of leisure. Life was so bizarre. Especially when you kept your heart open to new experiences.

"You're only old once." Her own words echoed back to her, clearer now than ever before. She did not wake up each day older than she was yesterday. She woke up younger than she'd ever be again.

❧ Chapter 3 ❧

WHAT WE CAN'T SAY OUT LOUD

Inside each of us is a little voice that tells us what we can and cannot say out loud. Even the cruelest sadist and the most obeisant masochist drew lines they would never cross in speech. Secrets of the soul that were swept into shadows of doubt and fear, truths that could never be revealed, longings that could never be externalized. But sometimes, the hidden cravings of a human heart emerged fully, not because we intentionally reveal them but in the ways we play.

Rosalie almost killed herself walking up the stairs. The wet palm of her hand slid on the handrail and she almost lost her grip. She panicked. Why the fuck was she here? She knew the minute she saw the building that she didn't want to go inside, but her phone beeped and told her to press the buzzer, so she did.

He was waiting. She had to go to him. It was now or never and she couldn't live with the idea of never.

She paused and steadied herself. He was up there. Waiting. She had to go. She walked mechanically, up a step and then, another, like a robot. Why was it so hard to walk up four flights of stairs? Oh yeah, because she was fat. Fat, fat, fat.

Would he think she was fat? Of course, he would. Everyone thought she was fat. Because she was. The mirror does not lie. Though sometimes she liked to tell herself that she exaggerated the flaws when she looked in the mirror, that, really, other people saw the attractive things. Her beautiful make-up and perfect fingernails. Her clean, lustrous hair. Would he notice them?

Anyway, her looks were irrelevant. She set her jaw. She was paying him. She was the customer. He was working for HER. He had no right to question anything about her. If he said one negative word, she was walking away with her dignity, and he could sue her if he wanted to get paid. Ha!

Her cheeks flushed, imagining the rage she would feel if he criticized her weight. She knew how to handle that kind of bullshit. She would kick his ass so hard he wouldn't know what hit him, sub or not.

By the time she was at his door, she was fit to be tied. Was he going to keep her waiting? Was that going to be part of his game? Pathetic.

She rapped on his door impatiently. A minute later, she tapped it more timidly. Why was she so mad on the day that she hoped would be the best day of her life? She rued the pounding she gave his door. She wouldn't open a door that was being knocked on like that. She'd be calling 911.

The door swung open. A tall, long-haired man in a long blue velvet robe stood before her. He looked like a wizard. All he needed was a pointy hat. He hesitated. Was he trying to decide if she was attractive enough to come in? She avoided his direct gaze. Big black leather boots stuck out at the bottom of his robe. If not for his height, he was like some kind of a hobbit, beard and all.

"Rosalie?" His voice surprised her. He sounded earnest and friendly. "I'm so happy to meet you, please come in." She thought Masters were all supposed to be mean. His words reassured her. He didn't look mean, he looked gentle. Her anger melted and her shyness took over.

"Yes... ummm." How should she address him?? He said his name was Lionel, Lion for short. "Master Lion?" she squeaked and dipped instinctively into a small curtsey. She didn't plan to do that. Oh, God, she was the dorkiest dork in Dorkville.

"Call me Daddy," Lion said with a smile, turning the door's numerous locks behind them.

"Oh," she shivered.

He took her hand as if she was a little girl and led her in.

It was happening. It was really happening. Her heart raced. The way he held her hand, the way she felt so small following in his giant shadow, it made her insides go *squish*. His shoulders were so wide! His back was straight and strong.

When they got to the living room, he put his arm around her shoulders, giving her a quick side cuddle. She felt like melting into him and vanishing.

"Would you like to talk for a few minutes before we go into..." he pointed at the door to another room.

She knew it had to be the playroom. She wasn't ready. "Yes, please!"

They sat down on the couch together. She looked at her feet and sat in silence.

"So would you like to tell me what brought you here today?"

"Oh my God," she said. "I thought I told you on the phone."

He smiled, then touched her hand comfortingly. "You did, but I was wondering if you wanted to tell me more about your fetish."

A shudder went through her. He said fetish so calmly, so easily, as if it was normal to have a fetish. That's not how she saw it! Other than their phone conversation, she'd never told anyone anything about what she called her little secret. Now it wasn't a secret anymore. She blushed scarlet red.

"I don't know if I can say it out loud," she half-whispered.

"Why's that, Rosalie?" She looked up at him in surprise.

"You know why! It's not something you can talk about to people. I've never talked to anyone about it, I mean... you can't talk about it. They'd think you were nuts."

"Doesn't that depend on the people you're talking to?" Lion asked.

"You feel I should be able to talk about it to you, right? That makes sense. I mean, I'm here." She turned her gaze back to her feet. The rug was nice, with cool colors that swirled into flowers and leaves. "I like the rug."

"Let's talk about you."

"Not much to tell. I have a job, an apartment, and some friends. Pretty standard, normal life. Oh, and I have a boyfriend, I guess I should have told you that."

"I appreciate you telling me, but I don't need to know about that."

"Maybe you do." She looked him in the eyes now. "I haven't told my boyfriend, actually fiancé now, what I'm into, ever. He doesn't know. I don't know how to tell him or even if I should tell him. I'm terrified. I really like him. I don't want to lose him."

"That's really sad." He looked genuinely concerned. It made her relax more. He was more human than she expected.

"You know how it is. It's the great unmentionable."

"I think we all need to talk about our true needs to someone," he said, caressing her hand. "And right now, that's me, right?"

She took a deep breath. "I guess."

"Let me prove it to you." He stood up and held out his hand for her to take. "Come with me, Little One. Daddy will show you."

She gasped and froze at that. He put his arm around her shoulders and gently led her, wondering and shy, into another room.

The first thing she noticed was an ornate bed pushed up against a window and a facing wall lined with intriguing things arranged in rows. Whips, paddles, gags, bondage thingies, chain thingies, lots and lots of thingies she'd never seen before. There was a whole section she couldn't quite comprehend: shiny metal cages, and giant dildos, so big she was sure they couldn't possibly be inserted anywhere. At any other time the thought of them being used on people would terrify her but she felt strangely relaxed and trusting.

"You won't use those on me, will you?"

"Oh no, you're not old enough for those!" he winked. "Have a seat," he gestured to a corner chair. "I'll make some tea. You do drink tea, right?"

"Oh yes," she said. "I love tea!"

"I thought you might. You look like a tea drinker. Take off your jacket. You can put it on the bed with your purse and shoes too. I'll be back shortly."

Rosalie felt awkward but did as he commanded. She wondered how many people had been on that bed. Would she be next? Or would he tell her to leave when she told him the specifics of what she wanted? She went to the chair and sank into it, her mind flying in a thousand directions.

How did he know she was a tea drinker? She could've been a coffee person. Everyone expected others to be coffee drinkers. She always felt weird being the only one to order tea when she was out with co-workers. Did she look like a tea drinker to Master Lion? What did that even mean? Then she remembered he told her to call him Daddy and her brain went blank.

The chair was unexpectedly cozy. She tried to reassure herself that he would accept her... thing. She hadn't been able to tell him exactly what she wanted over the phone. She tried, but the words wouldn't come. Nonetheless, he accepted the appointment. She stared at the instruments of erotic anarchy on the wall -- he had done it all. But had he done her things? What if it all went wrong? She hadn't even had time to think about that, she'd been so aroused by her fantasy of it all going right.

What made someone become a professional dominant anyway? You'd think a guy who looked that good would be a different kind of professional -- an actor or even a model. He was much better looking than she expected, though not quite as dashing as the headshot he posted online. In that photo, he wore sexy stubble and you could see his thick pink lips. Now he had a full beard. She wasn't sure how she felt about the curly scruff but decided that it worked for someone who was a daddy person.

She fixated on the wall of toys again. Knowing he wasn't going to use them, they didn't threaten her as much as they amazed her. How could there be so many different toys for making people feel pain? It was interesting that dozens, maybe even hundreds, of real people had been here, in this bizarre room. Did people scream and cry in here? No doubt about that. She felt herself get wet. She hoped he'd give her a safe word! She knew enough to know he should. If he didn't, she would leave!

Master Lion walked in with a tray and a ceramic Japanese tea set. It was so beautiful, it made her feel special that he'd bring it out for her. He'd shed the robe and she could see why he wore it to open the door. A leather chest harness gleamed on his bare chest. His large pink nipples were round like buttons. Light brown fur cascaded from collar bone to belt, his belly button barely visible under their soft curls. She imagined diving into that fur, getting lost in that fur. His black jeans were so tight you could see the bulge in his crotch. He was gorgeous! Her panties were soaking. She self-consciously crossed her knees. He was so good looking. Too good looking for her to be with in real life -- but she reminded herself this was part of the deal. She had paid to be awed by a handsome dominant man.

She tried to appear relaxed, but the most she could muster was stiff politeness and appreciative looks. She was afraid to move. She might knock over the tea set. When he handed her a cup, her hands shook so hard, he helped her lift it to her lips.

"I'm fine," she pulled away, steadying it with both hands. She gulped it. It was way too hot. Her lips burned, then her tongue, but she pretended it wasn't happening and swallowed the burning tea.

"Blow on it," he said.

She looked confused. Was he asking for a blow job?

"Blow on the tea, before you sip," he said.

"Oh! Oh, yes, I should."

"So why have you come to see me today, Rosalie?" He sat on a tall wood stool, looking attentive as if he expected a thrilling story. She was conscious of his head being two feet above hers. She wanted to curl into a ball and hide.

"Well, I..." she trailed off. This was the moment she'd been waiting for with all her soul and dreading with all her heart. "I was hoping you'd do my fetish."

He nodded. "Right..." He was waiting for more. She couldn't say more. She sipped more scalding tea.

"Can you describe what you want, Rosalie?" The repetition of her name made her jumpy. He sounded almost clinical like a doctor asking her to describe her pain level on a scale of 1 to 10.

"Well, I don't know how to explain it," she said. She knew exactly how to explain it, but suddenly she didn't want to explain it. Not to him, not to anyone. Her gut clenched up. Maybe this whole thing was a mistake. She didn't belong here, in this bizarre room with this dangerous stranger. What if he put something in her tea??

He continued calmly, "I got the sense that you're looking for a Daddy/girl type experience, yes?"

The sense? He got the sense?! She almost snorted. She told him that specifically. It was the only specific thing she'd given him. "Daddy/girl, if you know what that is?" she said to him on the phone.

"Yes," she tried to laugh in a friendly way, but the sound came out as a strange cackle. "Pretty much."

"What age would you like to be in this fantasy?"

"Oh," she said, then put the cup down. "Ohhhh... I don't

know. Whatever age you want me to be, I guess."

"I can't give you what you want if you won't tell me." Was he impatient with her already? Did she hear an edge to his voice. But he didn't look miffed. His eyes were so gentle.

"OK," she said.

They sat in silence for a moment.

"What age do you want to be?" he coaxed her.

"Young." That sounded so stupid she hated herself.

"How young?" He didn't seem to think it was stupid. He looked very interested.

"A little girl. A very little girl."

"Yes, but how little do you want to be, Rosalie? A baby? An 8-year-old? A teen?"

There was that clinical tone again! Was he going to analyze her fetish or do it?

"More... babyish."

Couldn't he tell that she needed to be held and cuddled like a baby? No, that would be unreasonable, too much. It was crazier to expect him to understand. She wanted to explain that she just needed to be held like a child. But the baby stuff, no she couldn't say that out loud. That seemed way sicker to her than the whips and giant dildoes other people came here for. The physical stuff was strange, but she knew that masochism existed. Her stuff, her fantasies and mind-games, that was the true weirdness.

"I see," he said.

Did he see? Did he??? She doubted it. But then he said something that pierced her to the core.

"You want to be a sweet little baby girl. Yes, that's what you want. It's darling."

She almost started crying. He did understand. "Kind of," she whispered. "But..."

"But what?" he prompted her.

Was he really going to make her say it out loud? That thing she kept fantasizing about but had never revealed to anyone. No one who knew her would ever in a million years guess her fantasy. Not even this man. She felt compelled to change the subject.

"Is Lion your real name?" she suddenly asked.

He looked bemused. "My real name is Corey. But to you, I am Daddy."

"Are you gay?" She felt like a fool for asking.

"I'm hetero-flexible," he said cautiously. He didn't look mad, just perplexed at the unexpected interrogation.

She'd never heard of hetero-flexible before. Did he mean he was heterosexual, but occasionally did men? Or did he mean he was gay, but was flexible about women? She didn't dare ask or he'd know how naïve she was.

"I guess you must see every kind of thing here, then. Every kind of person and every kind of fantasy."

"I've seen a lot," he said, steering the conversation back to their roles. "So tell me, Rosalie, do you want to be a little baby who poops their diaper?"

"OMG." She blushed to her roots. "Oh no, not that." The thought had crossed her fantasy mind a time or twenty, but she had convinced herself that it was what kinky people called a "hard limit." Besides, she could never ever poop in front of someone. That was simply too shameful.

"Pees their diaper?" He smiled. His smile transformed his face from someone cold and dangerous, into a sweet, caring guy, the kind of guy who rescues kittens and helps old ladies cross the street. She didn't know how she felt about that. What she had expected was a mean old sadist who wanted to hurt her. He wasn't old and he certainly wasn't mean. At least not yet.

"Well, no." She paused. Now she was outright lying. "I don't know. Maybe?"

"I see," he repeated. Her heart sank. He wouldn't do that with her now. Well, what did she expect, after all? He was a nice, normal-seeming man. But how normal could he be if he was doing this for a living? That wasn't very normal. Maybe it was normal in his world, but certainly not in hers. What would her co-workers think if they knew that she was here? Ice shot through her veins. It would be a nightmare. She would get fired.

He pointed to the bed and kneeled to unbutton her blouse when she sat at the edge. Now she could look into his eyes. What she saw thrilled her. He looked like the father who tenderly dressed his child in a movie she once saw. Only this wasn't a movie. She was living it. With a stranger who already knew more about her than anyone. She felt a pang of guilt. Her fiancé Phillip would never understand. Poor Phillip. He had no idea who he was marrying.

"Let's get you out of those ridiculous adult clothes, baby girl."

"Oh my god," she groaned, a tremor of lust suddenly electrifying her pussy. She was speechless. Her thighs were wet, but her throat was too dry to speak.

"Do you want to be a good girl for me, Rosey?" He removed her bra, ignoring her breasts and pulling her firmly against his chest until her breasts flattened under the pressure of his powerful hug. Such strong arms he had! She felt tiny in his arms.

"Yes," she croaked. "I do."

"Good, good," he stroked her hair. "Say, 'Yes, Daddy.'"

"Yes, Daddy."

He pulled off her skirt and then her panties, and got on the bed next to her. Now he moved her body onto his lap and wrapped his strong arms around her, like a daddy bear holding its cub. She went into a trance. A handsome Daddy was holding her tightly, cradling her in his arms. All the muscles in her body relaxed. Her insides went deliciously viscous as her anxiety evaporated, pore by pore. She felt soft and little and so feminine.

If this was all he'd ever do with her, it would be good enough. Just to come this far was a miracle. She felt safe. Safer than she'd ever felt with a man. Because this man understood. He understood and he accepted her. That made her feel frighteningly helpless and ridiculously grateful at the same time.

"Daddy," she sighed. "Oh, Daddy."

"Yes, little Rosey, you're relaxed now, aren't you baby??" He lightly stroked her hair.

"Yessss," she exhaled. Never had she felt this way. It was different from her fantasies. More satisfying. Her fantasy men were never this gentle. His gentleness cast light into the dark chaos of her mind. She'd never realized how much she needed a man to be gentle with her until now.

"I love your body, it's so curvy and ripe."

His words paralyzed her. She was so embarrassed she couldn't speak. He seemed to sense she was overwhelmed.

"Can you talk yet?" he asked.

She shook her head.

"OK, you can be my non-verbal baby. Would you like that?"

She nodded vigorously. Yes, she would like that. That's what she would like most of all. Not having to say things. Not having to explain or talk about it. Only to do and to be the person she had visualized so many times in her fantasies, the baby who didn't have to do anything except obey Daddy.

"The only thing you need to do is to let me know if something doesn't feel right and you need to stop. Your safe word is WAH." He grinned devilishly. "Let me hear you say it out loud."

She felt so silly! "Wah," she said.

"Louder," he coaxed.

"WAH!" she said as loud as she could.

"What a good baby," he said.

And then, things began to happen that she never believed could happen. He took his role seriously. He didn't mock her. He didn't pull away. He flowed naturally into his role. He was a miracle in her life. Blissful emotions flooded through her, a bliss she'd never experienced before. He knew what he was doing and he was good at it. She didn't have to say a thing. She didn't have to guide him. She surrendered to him. She surrendered fully, drifting and soaring as he provided all the dialogue. She'd never realized how much she'd hungered to hear the words he spoke.

"What a pretty little baby you are. I'm glad you're shaved and smooth, all ready for Daddy," he said. "Now I'm putting you in the diaper you should wear instead of those silly grown-up clothes. You'll look just perfect in a cozy diaper, my sweet girl."

A loud groan escaped her. She whimpered when he rubbed baby oil all over her shaved, sensitive pussy. He even powdered her! He knew exactly what to do and he had all the right equipment to do it. Her heart thumped as the inevitable finally happened. This moment she'd waited for her whole life. He made her raise her hips and then slid a diaper under her. It fit her perfectly! How did he even find one in her size!? The spate of questions vanished as quickly as they arose when he drew the sides together, closed the Velcro tabs, and sat back to smile at her once more. "Look how cute you are in that diaper," he said. "You are my sweet little baby."

She almost came right then. Her mind soared into an overwhelmingly erotic space she had never known before. Her mind was blank now, ruled by an intense state of arousal she'd never known, not with Phillip who she loved, not even when she was alone with her vibrator, creating mad fantasies to get off.

He knew exactly who she was. Daddy knew all her secrets. She was thunderstruck by how well this stranger knew her. It was as if he'd always known her, and always understood what she needed. He was omniscient. He really was her Daddy. And she was his baby. He wanted her to be his baby. He really truly wanted her to be his baby. She panted with rapture, unable to hold back her orgasm.

"Aww, I bet my little Rosey feels more relaxed now," he said. He rubbed the crotch of her diaper. "It feels a little moist down there. Did my little girl make a pee?"

"No, Daddy," she whispered. "It's my girl juice."

"Your girl juice," he repeated, biting his lip. "It smells lovely."

She inhaled shakily, so embarrassed, forcing herself not to cum. Then he reached into a pocket of his massive robe and removed a baby bottle filled with orange juice. Her excitement skyrocketed again, making her squirt in her diaper. When he offered her the rubber nipple she latched onto it hungrily. The juice was warm and sweet as nectar.

"Aw, little baby is so hungry." He slipped his other hand down to check her crotch again. "Your diaper is getting so wet, I may need to change you into a fresh one."

"I didn't pee," she weakly protested.

"It's okay if you do," he said, "that's what babies do. It's normal. I want you to. Can you make a pee for Daddy?"

The words sent her into another, even deeper space. Only faceless figures in her fantasies had ever said those words to her. He began gently rubbing her diaper right where it was the wettest. Daddy knew what she needed. The diaper crinkled and folded in all the right places, like a small blanket of electricity sparking explosions of desire. She couldn't hold back anymore. She came again and again, unable to stop coming for several minutes, rolling and moaning as he held her tightly and continued to feed her as she orgasmed over and over again.

He was giving her everything, everything she wanted, more than she dreamed she would ever have. She heard a strange noise and then felt something vibrating between her legs. He raised the speed until she began thrashing in arousal. A bolt of lightning convulsed her and made her scream. It was a full-body orgasm. A feeling she'd never had. Her. Little Miss Goody Two-Shoes, the straight-laced accountant on the third floor that nobody ever really saw.

She fell to the bed and hugged a pillow, subdued, depleted, in a calm place she'd never visited before. Never ever had she felt so relaxed. Without thinking, she filled the diaper with pee. She had no shame. No shame at all, not with him. She was safe.

"Is my baby all tired out already," he teased. He patted her diaper again. "Oh my, you're soaking wet. That's not all girl juice is it?"

She closed her eyes tight. "No, Daddy."

"Good."

She was thrilled at the word "good." He liked it. He approved of her acting like an infant. He understood her. And as if to prove that he did, he rubbed his hand over the diaper so she could feel her own wetness.

"Mmmm, oh yes, baby, you are soaked. Are you a happy

baby now?"

Happy! She rolled over to look at him and giggled. She felt happy!! Her! Happy! How crazy! She nodded.

"You are a good baby girl. Yes, yes, you are! You are a very good girl."

"Yes, Daddy, yes! I love you, Daddy," she cried.

"Awww," he said, then caressed her forehead and gently tucked stray hairs back in place. "Now Daddy will clean you up."

She was going to protest that she could take care of that, but he got to work like he was an experienced father. He swiftly pulled off the diaper, tossed it in a waiting trash bag, and cleaned her with baby wipes, back and front.

"Sweet and fresh again! Now let's take you back slowly to reality." He lay down beside her and massaged her shoulders and her neck, speaking to her in a calm and reassuring voice, telling her everything was okay, he was proud of her, and that she was adorable and sweet.

"Oh my God," she finally said. "I... I don't even know what to say." She didn't know how she would ever find the strength to stand up again. She felt like rubber all over.

"You don't have to say anything, little Rosey. Now is the time to come down from the baby clouds and feel the beauty and relief of what just happened here. Breathe in the happy and breathe out the sad." She inhaled deeply, and when she exhaled not a drop of sadness was left inside.

"I felt the relief. So much relief." She touched his face with her fingertips as if to make sure he was real. "Thank you, Daddy, thank you."

It had happened. It had really happened. Daddy had taken all the darkness away and replaced it with everlasting light.

⮞ Chapter 4 ⮜

LIVING YOUR TRUTHS

A single life is saturated with dozens of other lives, secret lives, old lives, fantasy lives, dream lives, the lives we could have chosen, the lives we hated living, and the lives we choose. Corey's journey took him from son to husband to father, from sub to slave to master, in an endlessly dimensional spiral into self-knowledge.

———————————————

When Corey saw his wife's name on his phone, he excitedly answered. He needed to talk to her, to tell her what he had learned today.

"Hello, darling!" he boomed into the phone. "I was hoping I'd hear from you."

"Hey, baby, just checking in with you to see how it went," Jax said.

"Good, good," he said, as he changed into his street clothes, hopping around on one bare foot and then crawling under the bed to locate his missing loafer.

"No issues, no problems?"

"No, not really. Well, right at the end, she told me she loved me," he admitted. "I don't know how to feel about that."

Jax laughed. "Yeah, that happens. Don't worry about it. Think of it as sex talk, Corey. It's what she needed to say as part of the catharsis."

"She had a whole lot of catharsis," he said. "Like so much. Catharsis! So many orgasms I lost track."

"That means you're very good at your job! Congrats. This Master thing is working out for you. I knew it would. Did you like her?"

"I did! She was very sweet and easy. Not much of a talker, but that worked well with the scene we did. I made her a non-verbal baby."

"Oh, non-verbal baby! I like the sound of that. I wish our babies were a little more non-verbal! Sounds like you pushed all her happy buttons."

"She was pleased. She even tried to give me a tip."

"On the stock market, I hope?"

"Ha ha, no. I told her my fee was sufficient."

"I would have taken the money."

"You're a bit of a Fin-Dom, aren't you?"

"Oh, we learned a new word," she said drily. "Where did you hear about financial domination?"

"On the Internet, of course, where else?"

"OK. Well, I prefer to think of it as embracing a client's spirit of generosity."

They snickered at each other, but Corey shook his head to

himself. He still struggled with the idea of grabbing for money, but he didn't judge his wife. How could he? He was living off her materialistic viewpoint. He was born bourgeois and became an art hippie. She was born wealthy, threw it all away and then built her own fortune from scratch. He didn't have the right to judge.

"By the way, I took your suggestion and put her in a diaper. It was so weird, but you know, it was familiar... just not familiar to do it with an adult, but she seemed impressed with my mad skills," he chuckled. "It was sweet, like a much gentler fetish than I ever tried."

"Right?" Jax said. "It is. It's kind of cute if you come to it with the right state of mind. I had a feeling that's what she'd want, especially when you said she wouldn't admit to any specific details."

"I thought her fetish was going to be a real problem for me," he admitted.

"The fetish is never the problem, it's people's shame about their fetish. The scene itself is pretty chill if you have compassion for them."

"It's a shame about shame. Ruining stuff for people, I mean. I felt so sorry for her. People come here and ask you to piss in their mouth like they were ordering breakfast. It's so amazing to me that people think pissing in a diaper is worse. Why?"

"My theory?" she said. "The less people understand a fetish the more they demonize it. She probably figured out on her own, maybe in painful ways, that most people wouldn't be receptive to doing it. They'd think she was a pedophile or something."

"Horrible." He put the wet diaper in a garbage bag and tied it tight. "It was just piss, no biggie. I cleaned up a lot worse in our kids' diapers! Remember that time Miranda's poopie shot out of the diaper and splattered a flight attendant? Holy fuck!"

"Oh my God, please no," she said. "I want to forget all those times."

"Stinkamole," he said, "like guacamole, but brown."

"Staahp!" Jax couldn't stop laughing. "Have you no pity? Several flight attendants were traumatized that day."

"They deserved hazard pay. That was some fucked up shit."

"You know, darling, you sound positively happy."

"I do?! Me, the second biggest grouch next to Oscar?"

"You mean the Muppet?"

"Yes, I mean the Muppet. Did you think I meant the acting award?"

"Ooh, you're feisty too! I think this whole Pro-Domming thing is doing good things for you, baby."

"You know what, baby? I agree. I feel, I don't know, re-energized by this job."

"Not a job," Jax corrected, "never a job. An avocation!"

Corey clicked on the video and grinned at her. She joined him in video. She looked beautiful as always, her skin soft and smooth as silk, her large grey eyes filled with kindness.

"That's a nice way to look at it. It does come from the heart. Definitely more fun than when I collected rocks."

"It's a service. Even when you're the top, you are always providing a service to a person in need."

He had always considered it a kind of slave service to his wife to take on the job. Now he had to sit down to process what she was saying. "You make it sound almost noble to spank and whip people."

"Well, isn't it?"

"That's hilarious. You're right, though."

"Aren't I always right, darling?"

"Yes, dear, of course you are. That's why I married you."

"You know what else I'm right about, darling?"

"Everything?" He loved sparring with her verbally. It reminded him of their compatibility, intellectually and otherwise.

"Well, that too," Jax said. "But right now I am being right about something else."

"What's that? Oh, hey, gotta shut the vid so I can finish cleaning and get out of here," he said, putting her on speaker. "What do you want to be right about now?"

"That you will take that wad of cash you earned and go to Zabar's. I am dying for some exciting fish! Trader Joe's failed me today. Cleaned out! And nobody's got toilet paper either."

"What kind of fish? The Nova or their smoked whitefish?"

"BOTH! Oh my God, both! The sliced Nova, please."

"The kids won't touch the whitefish because of the eyes."

"Even better!"

"Duly noted, Madame!"

He felt a surge of pride that he could afford to spoil her with expensive foods. Having his own money to spend was new and gratifying. He was grateful to her for encouraging him to try something new and different. He loved her beyond all reason. He loved her commanding ways when they played and he loved when she yielded to him during sex, going from stern to hungry. He loved her icy eyes and he loved her wild passions, and he loved her womanly curves. So many beautiful contours, so much sweet softness to curl up to on cold nights. The body that once harbored their precious children was made more beautiful to him by the lives she had carried inside her. Every inch of flesh was a testament to her inner beauty.

"Alright, my love, I've sanitized the last surface and I'm ready to hit the road and head to the Temple of Smoked Fish," he said. "I'll be home as fast as I can with bags of goodies for my Goddess. Bye, sweetheart, I love you."

"I love you so much, bye," she hung up immediately. He heard the click with satisfaction.

That was so Jax, to hang up after the first goodbye. She was a creature of authentic passion and firm boundaries all at the same time. It thrilled him to unravel her complexities. There were worlds inside of worlds in her body and mind. It thrilled him that he and he alone was the only one allowed to explore them freely. As cold and hard as she could be, she still gave herself to him completely when they were all alone.

Until he met Jax, Corey's dad was the only one who gave him the inspiration to grow his life and the freedom to quit lawyering to pursue his obsession with art. If his mother had her way, he would still be a widget in the Law machine, rushing to court half-cocked and half-conscious, competing with all the other suits carrying bursting briefcases for a victory that was seldom victory. Not when you dealt with the court system. Not when cases you won were lost on appeal by bigger, richer lawyers with richer, more corrupt clients. Lawyering was not the honorable profession he imagined it would be as a law student. Justice was an illusion. Instead of making him feel more moral, the court system made him feel dirty.

It was a miracle how Jax appeared in his life. He knew the minute he saw her on a deserted beach in Provincetown that she was the right woman at the right time. She was tall and self-possessed, with intense gray eyes that seemed to penetrate to his core when she stared back at him. He'd been ready to give up meeting a woman who was sadistic in sex play and endearing in real life until the moment she appeared. It was like he recognized her. A motor whirred, something clicked, and it was done. He fell for her so fast, it scared him at the time. But now he saw their meeting was fated, destined by a mischievous but generous god who saw two good people who needed each other. She needed to be fully loved by a devoted man; he needed to learn how to be free. She believed in him. She believed in his true potential. At first, he thought she wanted him to work as a prodom for the money. But these last three months showed him she had a higher purpose than putting her lazy bum husband to work. She wanted him to find new sources of self-confidence. She wanted him to know he had deeper resources than he'd imagined, that he could undertake new challenges and conquer them. She was so right. His creative block was a long period of stagnancy that ended the day he saw his first client. In dominating others, he connected with inner depths he never realized he had. There was a part of him that was a slave and sub to his wife, but there was also a part that craved to be in charge, to take on authority, to be powerful. He could feel the changes. He was becoming a better play partner, a better husband, father, and friend. He had a balance in his life now and he could choose which role suited which situation.

He did a final walk-through of the apartment. Everything was back in its place, order restored, bedding changed, the tea set drying in the kitchen drainer, bathroom toilet and sink wiped down with cleaner. He sprayed disinfectant everywhere and left.

The weather was beautiful, so he decided to jump on a bus to Lincoln Center and walk the rest of way to Zabar's and home. A good walk would give him more time to think.

He still felt the afterglow of his session with Rosalie. He wondered if the same mischievous god that brought him to his wife was still directing destiny, was somehow now leading him to become a Pro-Dom for the rest of his life. He could think of worse professions. Like the Law. Or art. How naïve he'd been to believe he was going to make a living as an artist. He had visions of accolades raining down on him, dreams of statues selling for big money, and a thirst for proving to the world he was a true artist. What a joke.

When his first New York City art gallery show was canceled, he shriveled up inside. He made so many sacrifices to line up that show, and for what? He tried to rationalize it, but he couldn't. He had wasted years of his life on a pipedream. He was done.

Fuck it all. Who cared about art when civilization itself was at stake? In two years, everything had spun out of control. All that work, all the years he'd put into it, all the nights he exhausted himself, all the times he didn't play with the kids, it all tore at him. What was the fucking point? No one cared about art during the plague. They cared about staying alive. Fuck, they cared more about finding toilet paper. Nothing made a person feel more like a frightened animal than going without paper to wipe their ass.

He hid in his studio and blamed COVID for ruining his life. Then, out of the blue, his estimable wife proposed that he work for her as a professional Dom. She owned three condos, leasing them by the hour to the people who worked for her. It was her own clever niche in an overpriced real estate market and far less likely to draw attention than a professional dungeon. She had five different people who made their own bookings and worked out of her 3 condos on a time-share basis. Each apartment looked innocent up front and had a back bedroom that she sound-proofed and turned into a dungeon.

At first, he resented her idea. Him, a Dom? His whole life he wanted nothing more than to worship a woman, to kneel at her feet and feel her power over him. He was born to be submissive, he argued with her. He would feel like an imposter dominating someone else.

But Jax said she saw his potential for giving people great scenes. He remembered trying to top some women in his dating days, when he was still too shy to admit that he wanted to be the bottom. He was such a failure at it! Still, he found it hard to tell her no. No matter how strange it might be for him, at least it would put some money in his pocket instead of depending on Jax's money. He hated being the hippie grifter who paid with his wife's credit cards.

Jax quickly tutored him on the basics of her business, explaining her protocols and company rules. He could share the condo Gigi had vacated with Marco, the other male dominant. That made it a little more appealing, since he and Marco were tight.

Jax gave him the same walk-throughs of the dungeon spaces and safety training she gave all her workers. She booked his very first appointment for him with one of Marco's regulars, who was delighted by the chance to break in a virgin Master. It was a standard session, the kind of tie and whip scene Corey had bottomed to a hundred times. He knew exactly how to draw the guy to the edge, then withdraw, and then take him to the edge again.

Afterwards, the client kneeled at his feet and said, "Are you sure you're new to this?"

He felt powerful that day, whole, more upbeat. And it kept happening. People came, he did unto them as had been done unto him and in two months, he had a small clutch of repeat customers. Pro-Domming was rewarding in ways he had never imagined. It felt like something that actually helped people. He wasn't half-bad at it. Ah, who was he kidding -- he was

KILLING it!

He got all the way up to 72nd Street, without finding a pack of toilet paper anywhere. At one store, the clerk laughed when he asked.

"Goddamn, man, is everyone hoarding?" Corey said in exasperation.

Then, in the window of a small bodega, he caught a glimpse of some off-brand paper and ran inside. Only one pack left, eight rolls for twenty bucks. Price-gouging in the Big Apple, he should have expected that.

"Yo, be happy," the clerk said to his sour face, "you got the last bag. Could be months before I get another shipment."

"Aw, shit," Corey said.

"My advice: use one sheet at a time," the clerk said.

"Do I at least get a bag?"

"Don't got no bags big enough."

Corey walked outside with the visible toilet paper, causing a small commotion.

"They got paper!" a passerby yelled, almost knocking him over as they ran into the store. A few others followed at his heels. He smirked, knowing he got the last bag. That was something anyway. The brave hunter had tracked down the last bag of ass-wipes in New York City. He was Master Lion and the Lion wasn't sleeping tonight!

Now if only he could transpose that masterly ego-state to art. If only he could feel that sense of pride again. That freedom to move by instinct and intuition, to trust his gut and take chances, and then see those risks pay off for him. To believe that his actions served some useful purpose.

He walked up to Zabar's and was greeted by the sharp

aromas of aged cheese and fish and salamis all merged into one nose-blinding bouquet. He usually shambled in, a little shy and embarrassed among the rich bitches and bastards cooing over the glass cases. Not today! He had scored toilet paper, the most valuable commodity in America! He saw a few envious looks and reveled in their jealousy. It must be awful to lead privileged lives and realize one day that you need toilet paper as much as the guy who cleaned the streets. He raised the toilet paper to his shoulder like a status symbol. Yeah, boy, he was the king of the ass-wiping jungle!

Fuck yeah. He was in a mood! A fucking great mood. And why the fuck not, Jax was the best wife a man could hope for, the kids were fantastic little people, and even the dogs were pretty cool. He had a wad of cash in his pocket that he had earned on his own, and a rare and precious commodity in the current state of the plague. And, he reminded himself, he helped a sweet, sad, needy woman feel a whole lot better about herself.

"Good evening, fellow New Yorkers," he bellowed.

Some people laughed, others look disconcerted, and Mario the cheese guy shouted, "Yo, Corey, you win the lottery?"

"I think I did, my friend," Corey shouted back, holding the toilet paper over his head like it was the holy grail. "Right?"

"Fuckin A," Mario laughed. "You de man."

∂ Chapter 5 ∞

WE ALL NEED LOVE

Human destiny comes in all sizes, shapes, capacities, and genders. Mistress Love learned through adversity that your body did not define you, your mind and your choices made you who you were. She released the demons of despair that once distorted her view of herself. She strove for self-love. She found her real family, a chosen family, who loved her strength. She knew now that by inhabiting her true self she became more powerful than her enemies had ever imagined she could be. Her greatest weapon against a hateful world was her clarity.

Mariangela smoothed her hair, applied a glob of gloss to her lower lip, pressed her lips together, then checked the results in her mirror. Perfect. She was hot as steak on a smoking grill. Juicy lips and dark lashes so long you could use them to glaze pastry. Dane was going to love her shiny lips! He'd better fall to his knees when he saw her.

The doorbell code sounded. It buzzed 2 times slow, 2 times fast, and ended with a final long buzz. He got it right for a change. Why the change, though?

She ran to the buzzer to let him into the building. She checked the clock. Right on time too. Evidently, punishing him for misremembering the code (twice) and showing up a little early, then late (three times), were off the table today. She remembered what Jax told her during training: "Improvisation and adaptation are the hallmarks of a skilled dominant." But why was he being so obedient today? It wasn't like him. He usually thought up some reason why she had to start punishing him the minute he walked in. Why wasn't he playing their sweet little kinky game today?

"Dane is here," Mariangela told the mirror, "your Dane."

She tucked a whip under her belt and went to greet him. When she opened the door, Dane stood there, a pitiful expression on his face. He didn't greet her with adoring words, he didn't smile eagerly nor dawdle timidly to be allowed in. "Hello, Mistress Love," he said dully.

"Are you okay?"

"Sorta," he said, walking past her, "not really."

He lay on her couch and buried his face in its cushions. She cringed. Jax assured her that the place was fully disinfected after each use of the space but still. Could there be germs still lingering inside the pillow? She yanked his hair to lift up his face, but he resisted.

"I need to rest," he mumbled into the couch, barely audible.

"You came here to rest?"

"Yes." The air stood still between them. "If you don't mind, Mistress?"

"Why should I mind, it's your money."

"Yes, Ma'am."

This was too weird. This was not a hotel. She spent so much extra time getting dolled up for him, too. Now he was playing possum on the couch.

What was his game? She always knew sooner or later he'd show his true nature. So, after all their years together, all his confessions of love, was this going to be the day he said he was never coming back? Was he going to pretend he was the real victim when he dumped her like hot trash? Yeah, she'd heard it all. Men! Couldn't trust a single one of them.

Maybe his witch of an ex-wife, Lucy, forced him to make this choice. How typical. He helped raise her daughter, Lizzy, and the kid called him Daddy. He loved that kid like his own. For her, he put up with the ex, even though she constantly found ways to insult him and put him down. He lived in terror that she'd find out he was seeing a Pro-Domme. She said she'd never trust him near Lizzy if he was "doing perversion again."

Mariangela's heart sank. Of course, he chose his kid over her. In her heart, she always knew this day was coming, that Lucy and Lizzy would end up destroying what they had.

Still, Mariangela remembered every promise he made. He told her she was the only one. The only one who could really fulfill him. She believed him like the idiot she was, even though she'd heard it all before, from a hundred different guys. Stupid of her to think Dane was different. He acted so decent. A Midwesterner with very nice manners and a soft demeanor. He was generous too, and always brought her presents. Sometimes flowers, sometimes a trinket from Tiffany's, he never arrived empty-handed. But today he did. He did not bring anything.

"Pay me now," she barked at him. She was renting the space, so she was not going to end up dumped and stiffed. She didn't know where this was going, but if he was going to spend an hour breaking up with her, it would cost him. She was tempted to ask for double!

"Oh yeah, sure." He stuck a hand in his pocket and held out a wad of cash in a rubber band. She slowly counted it up. All there. It appeased her a little.

"So, Dane, what is going on?" She tried to sound calm and casual.

"Lucy died."

"Oh no! Oh, Dane, I am so sorry!" she cried out. "When?"

"Last night. At the hospital. Couldn't even say goodbye, they wouldn't let us in."

"COVID?" she whispered.

"COVID," he said grimly.

She gently stroked his hair. "Oh, Dane, my poor baby. I can't imagine."

She didn't want to imagine. The horror of it. He came to her for comfort and she had such crazy thoughts. Relief washed over her, then a heavy twinge of guilt. She was glad the witch was gone, but still, what a terrible thing for the child to lose her mother. Mariangela knew what that was like. The kid was looking at hard times ahead.

She took a deep breath and sympathetically studied him. He was pathetic. He sure seemed broken up about a woman who did nothing but bring him misery. Now he could be with the kid and while it would be a burden for sure, maybe they could still have a happy life together. Or maybe not. She imagined the child's reaction when they met. Shock, maybe? Fear? You never knew how kids would react.

"There's more," his voice broke.

"There is? What else?"

"Her parents are taking Lizzy home with them to Rochester."

"What?! They can't do that, can they?"

"They were at the hospital with me all night and told me, flat out, that I have no legal rights to her since I never legally adopted her. They are named as her legal guardians and were prepared to fight me in court. I had no choice. They can give her a better life than I can as a single working parent. They have a big house and a beautiful farm. She loves it there, I know that. They said they'll put her in a good private school and she'll have cousins to play with and great family holidays. So I made the best decision I could for her and let her go home with them." He mashed his face into the pillow. "I don't know if it was the right decision. I'll never see her again! She'll forget I even existed."

"Oh my god, oh my god, honey, I am so sorry," she told him, holding his hand. She reassured him, "That was the right decision. You work 10-12 hours a day, that's no life for a motherless child." She stroked his cheek lightly and he purred. "She'll never forget you. You'll see. You can still visit."

Mariangela was struck by the depth of his grief over losing a child that was never his. It was strangely beautiful to her. He really was a gentle soul. His heart was big enough to love another man's child like his own. She wanted to put her arms around him and cry with him. But that wasn't her role. Her role was to make it all better. She couldn't give in to his grief. She was his sweet paradise. She had to heal him.

Dommes had to be prepared for emotional baggage, Jax told her during her apprenticeship. Jax had said, "Sometimes, your client needs you to hear and see them as regular human beings, not subs or slaves. But as fellow humans. They need to talk with you or cry with you, to let out things they couldn't tell anyone else because no one else knew who they were deep down inside the way their Dominatrix knew."

"Make room for me." Mariangela sat down on the couch, sliding under his face and chest until her lap made the perfect pillow for him. "Roll over so I can see your face."

He obligingly rearranged his body. His face was wet with tears.

"It'll be okay, honey, I promise, we'll get through this together." She stroked his cheeks gently. He started to wipe away the wet spots, but she gently caught his hand and put it back by his side.

"I'll take care of that." She bent over him and slowly licked his salty face, like a mama bear cleaning her cub.

"Oh my god," he sighed with surprise. "Oh. My. God."

"Does it feel good?" She lapped his face gently. "There," she said, "all gone."

"Oh, thank you, Mistress. Thank you. Any other day..."

"You would have been hard as a rock," she finished his sentence. "I know, baby."

He closed his eyes and for a second she thought he was going to fall asleep in her lap. He looked exhausted from all the trauma he just went through.

She lightly slapped his face. "Still with me?"

"Yes, Mistress Love," he said, eyes still closed.

"I don't think you really want to play today, do you?"

"Not really, Ma'am. I just wanted to see you. To be with you. Is that okay?"

"If you want to see me, open your eyes!"

The lids popped open. "Oh yes, Mistress. Oh, you look beautiful today. So beautiful."

"It's about time you noticed."

"Yes, Ma'am." He blushed.

"Do you know how much WORK it takes for me to look this good?"

He shook his head. "Ma'am, no, no, I..."

"Hardly any!" She cut him off.

He smiled weakly. "Oh, Ma'am, you are so funny."

She grasped his nipple through his shirt and pinched it roughly.

"What else am I?" she squeezed harder. He yelped. "Oh, it hurts, does it?" She pinched with all her might. "What else?!"

"You are cruel, Mistress," he gasped, "so cruel. You are terribly cruel, Ma'am!"

She eased her grip, then sat up straight again.

"That's right, slave. But you know what they say, you have to be cruel to be kind."

"Thank you, Mistress."

"What are you thanking me for?"

"For letting me come on such short notice," he said, "for being here. I had nowhere else to go." He choked on the words and tears started running down his face again.

A light in her soul switched on high! He wasn't breaking it off. He was running to her with an open heart, knowing she was the one who cared. She was his salvation. Her heart brimmed with joy.

"Ok, baby, we're good. I'll make you feel better. You know you're my best boy. I'll take good care of you."

"You will?"

"Of course. Mistress is going to make it all better."

He sighed deeply and she went back to stroking his hair.

Dane had to vent. For the first time, he told Mariangela all about his troubles with Lucy. She knew Dane was submissive when they got married, but then flipped the script when she signed the marriage license. No more kink, she declared, it was perverted and immoral, and she had to think of her kid. Dane was blindsided and betrayed, but stayed for three years, putting up with escalating abuse and insults.

Until he met Mistress Love. She was the one who finally liberated him from his shame about being submissive. She accepted him, she taught him it was okay. He finally got what he really wanted, a kind woman who gave him as much love as cruelty, a love without conditions or judgment. Not a non-consensual emotional sadist.

Then Dane said something that moved her. He told her that the money he gave his ex-wife came from the bank. But the money he gave to her came from his heart.

"You'll be okay, baby," Mariangela said, gently stroking his face again. "You're a strong guy. You'll get through this. We'll get through it together."

He stretched out in her lap, relaxing. She leaned over, bringing her mouth close to his, the lipstick so red her mouth was like a bright devouring rose.

"Mistress, may I call you by your real name today?"

"Sure, baby."

"Mariangela," he said, then repeated it again, "Mariangela. It's such a beautiful name. It's like a saintly name. Mariangela. My sweet angel."

"More like your sweet demon," she teased gently. She noticed his cock was stirring. "What do you need from me today, baby?"

"I need you to touch me," he whispered. "Touch me and make me feel alive. Please?" His eyes welled with tears again.

"Aw, you need love. I understand. We all need love. And I've got lots to give. That's why they call me Mistress Love!"

Mariangela rolled her hand over his mouth to silence him. She unbuttoned his shirt and pulled up his undershirt. She loved his chest. It was as furry as a poodle and just as soft. She leaned in and left a lipstick print on his belly, then helped him get out of the shirt and T-shirt. She began rolling his nipples between her fingers, in the way that always made him inhale sharply and throw his head back. She grinned.

They were so silent you could hear the kitchen faucet drip and the floorboards creak upstairs. They had their routine. Their place of quiet togetherness where her hands and his body created a magic that could not be put into words. It flowed noiselessly as calm waters, their energies meshing together as he writhed and gasped and her fingers aggressively explored. Her fingers slid into his underwear and grasped the head of his penis.

"This is mine," she said.

He groaned. "Yes, Ma'am, it is yours."

Their own special way of doing it wasn't like anything Mariangela did with her other clients. Dane was special. He was a sweetie. He treated her like a real human being, not a sex worker. He spent as much time talking with her as playing. She'd become his advisor and counselor on how to ask for a raise, how to handle the people who worked for him, and what to wear to important events. In return, he did everything he could think of to please her, taking her to nice restaurants and saving up every year to celebrate New Year's Eve with her just so he could kiss her at midnight.

He was such a good man. Loyal, kind, appreciative. He just

never had a mother who taught him to like himself. He was like a lost boy who needed a woman to give him the direction to go after the things he really wanted. No wonder he ended up with the ex. She was just as evil as his mother.

Dane suddenly grasped her little hands between his paws.

"Would you marry me, Mariangela? I know I don't deserve you but would you? Please?"

Mariangela reared back. "What??"

He slid to the floor and got on his knees. "Please marry me, Mariangela. Please make me a happy man!"

"I'm a little person," Mariangela said. "You don't want to marry a dwarf. Everywhere we go, every time people see us..."

"Stop! You aren't a dwarf! You're just petite!"

"Dane," she said sternly, "I'm the medical definition of dwarf."

"Oh, who cares what the textbooks call you. You're beautiful and strong and so smart and sane! You are beyond perfect to me! You're all heart, Mariangela! You're everything a woman should be! Lucy was conventionally pretty but her mind was evil and her heart was... a cold dead... cockroach." He held up his fingers and measured half an inch. "Not even this big."

"Dane! Don't talk like that about the dead. It's over now, you don't have to hate her anymore."

"I don't hate her," he said. "I hate that she held my life captive with her sick manipulations. Don't you understand? I am free now. I am free to marry you now. No one can stop me!" he exhaled like a dragon, releasing so much pent-up energy the room felt hotter. "I am free," he whispered incredulously. "I came here thinking this was the worst day of my life but it isn't. It's the best day. I am free to love you now!" He teared up. "You are the best human I've ever known. I want to spend the rest of my life with you."

She was flattered and flustered and so excited she had to stand up. "Dane, you really only know me as a Pro-Domme. I really only know you as a client."

"That's not true," he protested, grabbing her hand. "We know each other to the core. I mean, you know ME, the real me. The person I really am, and you know it better than anyone. You've told me that yourself."

It exasperated her that he was throwing her own words in her face, but it was also true.

"Let go of my hand. I need to process this," Mariangela quietly ordered.

She sat and he lay down, his head in her lap again.

"Close your eyes," she said. "I am taking you on a little trip."

She held him in her arms and caressed his face, and his hair, then drew circles around his mouth, walked her fingers around his neck, and swirled them through the hair on his chest. She thought the deepest thoughts of her life.

From the day she met him, she felt as if she'd always known him and that he'd always known her. It was just the details of their different experiences in life that separated them. Deep down, they had an energy she'd never known with anyone else, not even with Carmen or Jax, who had nurtured and mentored her, dried her tears a few times, and had her back at all times.

Maybe she didn't know everything about Dane, but she understood him. He told her that time and again. She alone understood him, he said. He appreciated her and respected her in ways no man ever had, and he allowed himself to be utterly vulnerable with her. The mutual raw honesty with each other was an unshakeable bond. She certainly knew his most precious secrets, ones he never dared tell anyone else. Even still, knowing the secrets of his sexual desires wasn't really knowing a person. Or was it?

Maybe it was. Maybe it was the best way of knowing him. She stared into the distance, wondering what Jax would say. Jax would probably think that getting to know a person's inner self was more authentic and intimate than only seeing their outer self. A childlike exuberance began to rise in Mariangela's spirit. Maybe they could make it together. How wonderful, how exciting, how... She took a deep breath and pushed the fantasies back down to re-ground herself in reality.

She always imagined herself marrying someone under 5'5" so they'd look more proportionate in public. Dane was a tall normie. He had a few extra pounds on him but was still very athletic for his age. He swam, he lifted weights, and he looked great in a suit. He was going bald, but his eyes were beautiful and his jaw was strong. When he hugged her she felt so relaxed, so safe. He had a great cock too. More importantly, he treated her like a queen.

Sure, they would look funny walking together. They'd never slow-dance together -- her nose only reached his belly. Bad enough that strangers constantly made rude remarks to her, now they'd be a regular comedy act. She cringed when she thought of how the Internet would turn them into a meme if they were ever photographed on the street.

Dane had been coming to her for two years now and never once said anything that pissed her off. Pretty amazing considering how hot her temper was! But Dane, he was always a good boy, a good man, always kind to her. She remembered their first session together. He explained it was just a one-time thing and apologized profusely, explaining that his custody situation prevented him from seeing anyone regularly. Yet he came back two weeks later... and the week after that. Then he never stopped coming back every week. Even today, after losing his wife and child, he rushed to her door.

He needed her. No man ever needed her as much as he did. She knew that. She knew she had the power to make him happy. And he made her happy, so happy she'd broken all her own rules and had sex with him. Great sex. Beautiful sex. So fuck the haters. Fuck them. Haters would hate them for being BDSM too if they knew. Would that make either of them any less kinky? No! They deserved to live their passions together. Marriage was about how they felt for each other, not what idiots said about them behind their backs. Still, was it fair to subject Dane to their mockery? Shouldn't she protect him from the way assholes acted when they saw her? Did he even know what he was getting into, how stupid and cruel people could be?

She kept stroking him gently, now extending her range down his chest, unbuttoning his shirt to expose his nipples and teasing them lightly.

She had been waiting her whole life for true love. Now the right man had asked the right question in the right way. She stroked his cheek, lost in thought.

Dane sighed and smiled, at peace in her lap.

"You are so good to me," he said, closing his eyes to bask in her long caresses.

"And you've been wonderful to me, Dane. Give yourself to this moment, baby," she said. "Let Mistress Love's heart fill your soul."

"Yes, Mistress, I feel your love in my soul."

"This could be our forever," she murmured.

"I want a forever with you," he whispered. "I've never wanted anything as much as I want to build a life with you."

"OK then!" she said, kissing his soft lips.

"Wait?" He opened his eyes and stared hopefully into hers. "What do you mean?"

"I mean yes."

"Yes? YES??? You mean yes?!" He trembled with joy. "You'll marry me? Oh, my darling Mistress, am I dreaming?"

"Yes, I said yes, yes, I will marry you. Now shut up and let me love you forever."

❧ Chapter 6 ☙

WHAT IT'S ALL ABOUT

Corey drank his fill from the river of life. With each new experience as a dominant came new revelations about the true diversity of inner lives. He was a student all over again, thriving on complex power dynamics, eager to forge new pathways to emotional fulfillment and to indulge even the strangest requests. He abandoned his foolishly rigid notions of right and wrong about sex. There were only things that lifted a person up and things that kicked them down. He chose to lift his clients high and to let each success motivate him to accept himself with the same kindness he showed them.

Stan was a short, wiry guy with styled and sprayed, dyed blond hair that glistened over his bald spots. He wore a baby blue jacket and a white shirt with too many open buttons. If you were following him down the street, you'd notice that his shoe heels were unusually high. It gave his gait an odd aspect, as if he was playing kick the invisible can. If you were to look inside the shoes, you'd realize there were lifts in addition to the heels.

Stan was not tall in height, but he was in tales. He was a salesman who had relentlessly honed his skills in front of the mirror in what he called "my bachelor pad." It was a modest but tidy, boring, yet cozy apartment in an undistinguished, yet respectable white building on Manhattan's Upper East Side. It had a lovely, glittering lobby but no concierge. Had there been one, you can be assured that Stan would have been his best friend. He also would have gifted and then sold vitamins to his friend.

Stan had what was called "the gift of gab," and his brain gabbed even faster than his mouth. He was an immigrant to Manhattan from the lost paradise of Sheepshead Bay, Brooklyn. If it had been a real paradise he might have lived in his parents' basement until they died. But Manhattan had summoned him, with its adult playgrounds and opportunities for endless romantic adventures. He went everywhere. He did everything and everyone. He'd fucked men in dark alleys, done women on rooftops, and let transwomen take him wherever they wanted because he loved them. He'd been to uptown orgies with expensive chandeliers and low-end brothels with roaches on the walls.

Ever since COVID began, he was lucky if someone showed up on the other side of a greasy glory hole on Desperation Row. He thought it was pathetic that people were staying home. He built himself a true survivor's mask. With a helmet to protect his upper face and a respiratory mask he further padded with gauze, he steered through the streets of New York feeling invulnerable. Behind his cage of plastic and glass, he sneered at people in fabric masks.

He reached in his pocket for the address he wrote on a

scrap of paper. He was meeting up with a dominant guy from the Internet. He never thought he'd have to pay for sex but in these times, and with this economy, everything came with a price. It really burned him that a man like him should have to pay for a commodity that he always got free. He always scoffed at people who paid for sex and now, here he was, lowering himself.

He spotted the building and went inside. The lobby was old and crappy. He should have known. He considered ditching but he'd been fantasizing about the guy since he saw his ad, and he was already half-hard, just walking here. He sighed and climbed the stairs to the guy's door.

The guy who opened the door looked like a hippie with long hair. Stan's heart sank. The photo he saw was a guy with stubble and much shorter hair, more like a yacht owner than a cab driver.

But it was too late now, and he'd had a lot worse. At least the guy's hair looked clean. His fingernails too. So Stan gave him his sales smile and stuck out his hand.

"Nice to meetchyah!" he said. "I'm Stan. Stan the Vitamin Man. But I'll save that for later."

His host took his much smaller paw in his own and shook it firmly.

"Hey, yeah, that's quite a grip you got there." Stan looked around the apartment and relaxed a little. "So are you Lion or Lionel?" he asked.

"You may call me Sir," Corey said.

"Ok, Sir Lionel, I see you got some nice stuff here, cool, cool." He gazed admiringly at the chintz armchair and the elegant reading lamp beside it. "My grandma had that chair."

Corey, who had found the chair on the street and

meticulously restored it, almost said, "It could be hers," but held his tongue. He didn't have a handle just yet on Stan, who struck him as both droll and almost unbearably chatty.

"What kind of vitamins do you sell?"

"Oh, supplements. A lot of Kratom. Did you know it's about to revolutionize human health? I'll leave you a sample later."

"I see." Corey shrugged off the robe and let it drop to the floor, walking away like a diva. "Let me show you to the dungeon," he said.

Now Stan felt a resurgence of blood in his member. Beneath that ugly robe Lionel was buff! Hot Daddy buff, with a high juicy butt Stan wanted to lick. OK, this was more like it!

Corey stopped at the doorway to the next room. Stan peered inside like a spinster looking at a Honeymoon Suite.

Stan was impressed. It was clean and very classy! Lots of expensive toys. This guy really spent on toys. Well organized, too! He took special note of the butt plugs. He had considered a reaming. It was COVID-safe, he reassured himself. And he was in the mood to be reamed by a hot Daddy. He felt instantly better. Maybe this was worth it, after all. You didn't see this kind of set-up every day. It made Lionel seem more professional, what with the charmingly furnished front room and the exceptional back room.

"It's a hidden den of depravity in the middle of a family neighborhood," Stan said. "Gotta love it! Good job, Lionel!"

"Please call me Sir, Master or Master Lion," Corey said patiently.

Stan grinned. "OK, sure, I'll call you Master Lion. It's a good handle. Could you call me Little Stannie?"

Corey nodded. "Take off your shoes." Stan hesitated.

Corey said, "Take off your shoes, Little Stannie."

Stan grinned again and removed them, his height now shrinking about 5 inches. Corey took the high-heeled shoes out of Stan's hands. He was dying to examine them closely to see how Stan had masked the lifts, but he didn't want to make the guy act even weirder, much less get offended. Corey loomed over him. He felt like a giant. Stan was hard as a rock checking out the expensive looking harness outlining Corey's tits and abs. He always had a fantasy about being taken by a big man and Lionel was a BIG MAN, with big dick energy. Stan's dick strained against his pants, aching to be released.

Lionel didn't ask him to take off his pants. He grabbed the waistline and pulled it hard, almost lifting Stan off his feet like a ragdoll. Stan surrendered immediately.

"Oh, Master," he trilled, "you are so strong."

Corey unzipped his fly and pulled his penis out.

"I see you are already prepared to get a workout. Take those socks off and follow me." He walked to the wall.

Stan eagerly pulled off his socks and hopped after Lion. That ass was so delicious, he'd follow it anywhere. Corey stopped at the first section of implements lining one wall.

"Do you like cock bondage?" He held up a metal cage and Stan smiled.

"It's a beauty, but not for me."

Lion walked to a selection of paddles and whips of every kind. "Do you need punishment?" he asked. "Have you been a bad boy, Little Stannie?"

"I probably do," Stan said, letting the phrase "Little Stannie" wash over him, enjoying the way Lion said it, real deep and sexy, almost affectionate in a way. "But, nah, not really, though I do enjoy a spanking now and then."

He could see in Lion's eyes that he was not getting the

responses he wanted. "So," Stan said, "what about those butt plugs?"

"What about them?" Lionel bowed his head with a coy smile. "Do you like them?"

"Doesn't everyone? Hey, what's the biggest one anyone's taken? I bet you've seen it all!"

Lionel walked to a monstrous pinkish-flesh-colored cock as long as his arm.

"I call this one my second in command," Lionel said. "The subduer."

Stan burst out laughing. It was a huge motherfucker of a dildo. He bet anyone would be subdued with that monster rammed up his ass.

"OK," he said, unbuttoning his shirt. "I'll try it."

Lionel hesitated. He thought he'd be intimidated by it, not ready to get rammed by it. Stan was such a small man! "Are you sure you want me to put that inside you?"

"All the way!" Stan said, then obligingly added, "All the way, Jose. I mean, Master Lion."

Corey froze in surprise. Yeah. Stan had seen that look before. Just because he was a short dude didn't mean he had a little hole. He knew how to stretch as well as any big guy. And with the right guy, he might be able to stretch more than he ever had. He got the feeling Lionel was the right guy.

"You'll use a lot of lube, right?" he asked.

"Of course," Corey replied, snapping on a pair of latex gloves. I can go traditional with Crisco or contemporary with the water-based kind."

"Ha! You do it old school! I love it," Stan yipped. "Jesus that brings back memories. I haven't seen a blue can around in years.

But nah, I'll go with the new stuff, it works much better for me, easier to clean too."

Corey went to the industrial-sized container of lube and Stan instantly recognized it from Amazon. "You really spare no expense!" he babbled. "I love it."

"You think I got enough here for you?" Corey teased.

Stan laughed and his dominant chuckled too. Suddenly they were just two bros having a good time and about to have a better time. Stan gave him a keen lustful glance. This dude was hot AF. Nice guy! Big bulging arms, big chest, tall, hairy, and his dick looked huge in his tight pants. Real Tom of Finland type. He would look better with a crew cut, but the long hair worked on him somehow, like a real lion's mane. Grr! Lionel was a beast! This was working out even better than he expected.

Stan slid out of his mesh underwear and dove onto the bed, ass up. Soon his top was right behind him, touching his ass with a bare hand, giving it a few light spanks.

"Ooooh, yes, Daddy, that feels good." Stan squirmed. "I guess I was a bad boy."

Lion's voice got low and guttural. "Of course you're a bad boy, Little Stannie. You're a greedy boy. You want what big boys want. But can you handle what I'm about to give you?" The slapping got harder.

Lion covered every inch of Stan's pale cheeks and thighs with a firm hand. Firm, but not unfeeling. He massaged between strokes to relax the muscles. His cheeks seemed to part like the Red Sea when Lion's palm smacked it. Stan got a little self-conscious. His ass wasn't the chiseled plum it used to be. Lionel obviously didn't care. He was spanking that ass like it was made of gold. Stan felt a twinge of gratitude about that. Made him feel hotter!

Stan squealed with delight. "Oh, yeah, oh yeah, Master, I'm a bad boy, I'm a really bad boy. I deserve to be fucked up my ass so far I can taste it in my mouth!"

"Are you sure a boy like you can handle a toy made for a big man?"

"Yes, Master," Stan cried in delight. "I can handle it. You wouldn't believe how good I'm going to handle it. I want to handle it for you, Master. Make me handle it for you, Master, take me to the limit!"

"Alright, Little Stannie," Lion said gruffly. He roughly pushed Stan's head down onto the bed. "You're going to handle it for me. You're going to take every inch of my huge butt plug up your hot hole." Then he said, "Your safe word is bussy."

"Oh my God," Stan cried, then he said, "I hope I'm not too little for you, Master. I don't want to disappoint you now. That would be terrible, to disappoint a hot top like you!"

The game was in full swing now and Corey was getting into it almost as much as Stan. He lowered his voice to a calm rumble. "I'm not going to let you disappoint me, Little Stannie. I'm going to make you take it. It's going so deep inside you, I'm gonna check your mouth to make sure it isn't poking out."

Stan wailed into the bedding, trapped between fear and desire. He felt Lionel apply the cold lube to his hole, working it expertly, opening Stannie like a can of beans.

"Go on, boy," Lion said, his fingers gliding inside, slowly. Stan pushed his hole onto the fingers, lusting to suck Lionel's whole hand inside. "Yeah," Lion said, "you're an ass-slut, aren't you." He slid his hand into the hungry hole. "You're just a greedy hole."

"Oh my gawd," Stan groaned in ecstasy. "Oh my gawd, I didn't even tell you."

Lion paused. "Tell me what?"

Stan whispered. "Please call me hole, Master, tell me I'm nothing but a hole to you."

"Ah! Well, that is what you are." Lion resumed probing and gently pushing his hand inside up to his wrist. "You're nothing but a gaping hole for me to fill. I'm going to open that hole wider and fuck it harder than you've ever been fucked, and I'm going to use the biggest dildo you ever saw."

"Yes, Master," Stan gasped, "I deserve the biggest dildo."

As quickly as he eased his hand out of Stan's ass, he inserted the slippery head of the monstrously thick, long rubber dildo into it. He slowly and cautiously moved it inch by inch, expecting some natural limit to push back. Instead, the dildo went in deeper and deeper, as if Stannie had no internal organs, just a huge cavity ready to be filled. Finally, Stan winced and Lionel realized it was all in, right down to the flared end.

"Impressive, you whore," Corey muttered. "Little man, big asshole."

Stan writhed at his words. Lionel rocked it carefully inside him. The silence in the room exaggerated the distant noise of car traffic. It was just another day in New York, where mainstream life proceeded at its standard hectic pace, while behind closed doors, people led secret lives of shocking behaviors.

Stan was in another world now, panting and sweating but utterly silent, lost in the private sensory deprivation tank of his own mind, where nothing but his asshole was fully conscious. It took a lot of focus to deal with the mammoth toy in his ass.

Corey kept speaking in a stern but calm voice. "This is what you deserve, Little Stannie. You're my ass-slave now. My pussy-assed bitch. My personal hole to stretch and fuck at whim." He made a soft growl at the slave beneath him.

Stan soared into deep space. Corey watched him go, his eyes rolling back in his head, his body twitching uncontrollably, almost like he was in a deep sleep. For Stan, it was a place of ultimate peace: there were no racing thoughts, no anxiety, no self-consciousness, just a monster dildo stuffing him like a pinata, making him sweat and groan and surrender to the powerful master who knew exactly what he needed. Now he was who he really was, and he was over the moon. He was an ass-fucked faggot getting cornholed by a man strong enough to kill him, but who chose to ream him with great care and attention, almost like he really liked him.

This Lionel dude was so good. So fucking good. Like, eager and invested in giving him the best time ever. He was even passionate. Stan couldn't resist him, couldn't fight him. It was the feeling he had always wanted to have. A feeling unlike any other. Words couldn't describe it. He shrieked as the semen spurted out of him. He'd never shrieked in his life but it was like he couldn't stop. Then he shuddered so hard he thought he'd fall off the bed -- but he couldn't go anywhere, he was nailed to the bed by the dildo, by the Master, by the predicament. To his surprise, he squirted again, another smaller load that drained him completely, something that he'd never experienced before.

At last he went so limp, he looked like he was in a coma.

"You okay, Buddy?" Corey asked.

Stan couldn't speak. He didn't want to. It would break the mood. He wiggled his fingers to signal he was okay.

Corey decided to let him recover at his own pace. He slowly pulled out the dildo. It came out with a little pop, and some lube drooled out. Corey dropped a fresh towel on him to clean up and carried the toy to the bathroom to wash and sanitize it.

When he got back, Stan hadn't moved.

"Hey, Stan, are you okay?"

"Mmmmmph."

"What?"

Stan bolted upright. "I'm fine. It was good. Thank you very much. You really know what you're doing." His clothes flew back on him as quickly as they'd dropped off. He also patted his pockets to make sure his wallet and cell were still there. "Good, good. Everything is fine." He pulled out a couple of hundred dollar bills and dropped them on the bed. "Two hundred, right?"

"Yes, that's right. Thanks."

He was about to offer a hug and do his aftercare routine, giving the man a light massage, accepting some kisses, speaking in a soft gentle voice to help Stan come down. But Stan just jumped into his shoes and hurried to the door.

"Wait," he called after him. "Don't you want a hug?" He always offered aftercare and clients always accepted the offer, gladly. Stan never even asked for his real name.

Stan turned around. "Nah, man, I don't do hugs. I gotta get back to real life now."

"Oh," Corey glanced at his phone, "you work nights?"

"I'm not going back to work. I'm going home to the wife. She's making pot roast tonight. I never miss pot roast night."

"You're married? To a woman?"

"Hell yes, I got a wife. Does that surprise you?" Stan asked. "My bachelor pad is for sex, but I go home to wifey every night."

"Nothing surprises me," Corey said cavalierly.

"She was my high school sweetheart! We've been together 28 years. 28 great years! We got six kids!"

"Good for you," Corey said. "Sounds like a great life." He

wasn't exactly lying but he was flummoxed.

"See you next time," Stan called over his shoulder as he dashed out of the dungeon, then out of the front door, and far, far away from everything that had just happened.

Corey needed to lie down. This was too much. Not physically, but mentally. Stan had exhausted him. He went to the small closet at the back of the dungeon and removed a leather cape that his wife bought for him the time the boiler broke down. He almost froze his ass off during a scene in a leather jockstrap and harness that cold winter day. Now he always kept a thick robe handy and used it to greet people so he didn't have to open the door in his work gear. The cape, though, proved more versatile. He practiced flaring the soft leather like it was Dracula's own cape. It gave him a powerful, almost supernatural feeling that worked really well with a couple of clients who had vampire fantasies.

He carried the leather cape to the couch and spread it on top of himself like a blanket. He was in his little Batcave now. Dark and serene with that sweet musky smell of leather. What was it about that smell that always made him feel so primal, so connected to his own senses? He grunted in satisfaction, inhaling it until he felt more whole.

He needed to analyze what happened with Stan. For the first time since he'd been working, he left a session feeling bewildered. Not that Stan was straight, though Corey had been 100% sure he was gay. Not that Stan ran out like a dog escaping a dogcatcher. It was more the feeling that he'd just dominated a real-life shapeshifter. Who the fuck was Stan? What was he about? He was the deepest sub he ever met but only when the dildo was up his ass, otherwise he was a manipulative son of a bitch with control issues. He was the gayest gay guy except he wasn't gay. Or at least he didn't identify as gay. Or didn't think of himself as gay.

Corey wondered what his wife thought about him. With six kids, maybe it never even occurred to her that he was anything but heterosexual. Was that possible? Yes, yes, anything was possible. It was even possible she knew all about his strange fetishes and hook-ups, and accepted them, as he did, as some kind of side hobby, like birdwatching or stamp collecting, something just odd enough not to want to be involved with but not odd enough to bring a divorce suit.

If Stan wasn't gay, who was? You saw it in the news every day -- the anti-gay politicians who got caught cruising men's toilets, the viciously homophobic preachers who were busted for having gay affairs. If Stan was straight, why did he train his asshole to act like the Mariana Trench?

Corey pulled the cape down and breathed in fresh air.

The only thing Corey felt sure about was that whatever his orientation, Stan gave himself fully to a total stranger, and let that stranger take him on a savage journey.

In all the years he'd been married, Corey had never been able to surrender power the way Stan surrendered to him. He wondered what allowed Stan to trust a stranger so completely. He flashed back to Rosalie. She too had surrendered completely to him, which seemed paradoxical since she could barely talk about what she wanted without turning bright red. How did they do it? How did they throw themselves into submission when submission was their dirty secret? What kind of emotional disconnect, what kind of wound, allowed them to live as two completely different people in the one life they had?

He picked up his phone and called Marco. Marco would have answers for him.

"Yo, man," he said when Marco picked up. "Got a minute?"

"For you, darling? Of course I do. What's up?"

Corey quickly spilled the dirt on his session, start to finish.

"You used the monster?!" Marco's eyebrows flew up. "Wow. Nice!"

"I didn't just use it, the dude's ass literally sucked it up like a vacuum."

"Ohhh, HOT!" Marco said. "Jeez, if you don't want him, send him my way!"

Then Corey told him Stan was married with six kids and didn't think he was gay. Marco nodded, as if he'd heard that story a thousand times. Maybe he had.

"It be that way sometimes," he finally said.

"Do you think he's gay, though, and in denial?"

"I think he's whatever he identifies as," Marco said. "I wouldn't question it. If he thinks he's straight, he's straight. I mean, the whole world might think he is gay because of him having a gay scene with you, but... Come to think of it, you did that scene with him and you're not gay."

Corey flung the cape over himself again. "Well, okay, you have a point but..."

"But what? People aren't obligated to fulfill other people's definition of what is gay or not, right?"

"Riiiight," Corey said, "True..."

"Don't sound so skeptical, my friend. There are no rules. You have to accept that sex is weird and messy and often ambiguous. Hey, I fucked your wife and I'm gay, right?"

"And you sucked my dick, but I'm het," Corey conceded.

"Exactly. Who we can have fun with doesn't necessarily define who we are."

"I guess." Corey still felt tentative. "But, seriously, isn't he gay?"

"Maybe a little." Marco lit a joint. "Maybe clinically. I don't know. But if he thinks he's straight, it's the least you can do to just accept his definition and move on. Otherwise, trust me on this, you will stumble into a world of hurt defending your position on the Internet."

Corey choked. "Yeah, not going there, not going to argue with anyone on the Internet about what constitutes real homosexuality."

"Wise choice."

"So you don't think he was weird?"

"Oh hell, I didn't say that!" Marco laughed. "He sounds like a total freak!"

"He was a freak!" Corey cried. "I mean, the whole thing was surreal, from him pretending to pass out so he didn't have to talk to me and then checking his pockets to make sure I hadn't stolen his wallet when he was in that cum-coma. Jesus Christ. So fucking strange."

"Cum-coma," Marco repeated. "Oh my God, Cum COMA. I'm going to use that someday."

"Thanks for the talk," Corey said. "I'm confused as fuck but feel a lot better now."

"Oh good, I've totally not resolved a thing for you! You're so welcome."

"I love you, man."

Marco nodded. "And you're not gay."

"Alright, alright, I get what you're saying. I'm just saying..."

"Goodbye? Because you have to get home to your wife after ass-fucking a dude with King Kong's ding dong?"

"Fuck," Corey couldn't stop laughing. "Fuck you and goodbye."

"Till we meet again, Batman!"

Corey shut the phone and dove back under the cape.

It was the strangest experience ever, fucking bizarre shit that made his brain hurt, but after talking to Marco, he felt exhilarated. Now he just had to figure out how to give himself to Jax the way strangers gave themselves to him.

✌ Chapter 7 ✿

WE ARE WHO WE ARE

A family of the heart is the one who doesn't have to love you because forces greater than themselves made it so. They choose to love you. They don't see you as a burden, but as a treasure. A family of the heart recognizes your value as a human being and allows you to live your truths without judgment.

"**W**hy are you wearing that floral horror?" Carmen cast a sharp eye on Lo's dress.

"Don't mock the dress. It's not for you," Lo huffed. "It's for the Dunhills."

"Oh no. The people with that little barfy baby?"

"Yep." Lo smoothed the dress over her hips, then pulled her hair back tightly and tied it. "The flowers will hide any puke. I have a court appearance with them today so I may have to hold her for a bit. Solid colors are off the fashion menu."

"I don't know how you do it, my beauty." Carmen shook her head. "Barfing babies are a hard limit for me."

"Oh, Ma'am," Lo tittered. "It's not that bad, really."

Lo was a Social Worker. Poverty, addictions, screaming spouses, neglected children, all the sorrows of life were her job to mediate and repair. With her heart-shaped face and caring brown eyes, Lo carried her burdens with a calm dignity that gave comfort to all she met. Carmen admired her patience and forbearance, her ability to stand up to challenges that others avoided, and her quiet determination to make a positive change in the lives of the needy, the lost, the outcast, and the marginalized. Lo never gave up hope that the world could be a better place.

Carmen loved her wife but was not envious of her job. Carmen was an art appraiser who navigated a plush and decadent world of wealthy art investors. She glided through their insulated lives with ease, but her mission in life was rescuing great art from obscurity. Nothing made her happier than sorting through buried treasures in attics and basements and sometimes in dusty closets and beneath floorboards. She was meticulous, organized, diligent, and passionate in her work.

She wore a standard uniform every day: loose fitting black pants, a long-sleeved silk shirt, flat Gucci loafers, and a signature gold necklace that Lo gave her to signify Carmen's power and precision. It was a shiny little gold sword that glittered with every step Carmen took.

"For my warrior goddess," Lo said when she presented it to her Mistress on their first anniversary. Fifteen anniversaries later, Carmen still touched it tenderly in the mirror every morning with joy.

Over her seeing-rich-people uniform, she wore a second one for her jaunts to artists' homes. It was a loose gray jumpsuit she zipped up over her clothes, with latex gloves, a blue painter's cap, and a face mask so she could crawl down into a sub-floor or climb into cobwebbed attics. It delighted her to hunt down forgotten works of genius, and she felt elated when her finds drove investors into feeding frenzies at uptown auctions.

"Are you sure you wouldn't rather be a stay-at-home artist with a sugar-Mommy?" Carmen asked her wife. "Business has been picking up, and I'm feeling pretty rich right now. You could take a break."

"Nope. I'm GOOD at this," Lo said.

"I know are, sweetheart," Carmen said. "You are really good at it. But you could be good at less stressful things. You could finish your history degree, for example."

"Why go back in time when the present needs so much help?" Lo said, her usual response whenever Carmen tried to nudge her back to graduate school. "Besides," she said, trying not to sound too excited, "there's a rumor that I'm up for a big promotion!"

"Awww, honey, that's fantastic. I'm proud of you!"

"It's just a rumor." Lo shrugged. Then she beamed. "But, yeah, I know! I'm up for executive director!"

They grasped each other's hands and Carmen danced her around the room.

"You know, I have to get to work," Lo finally said, pulling away.

Disappointment flowed through Carmen. "Really? You couldn't be a little late today?"

"Oh no, Ma'am, no I can't. Court date, remember." She smoothed the floral horror. "Got my armor on." She grabbed her briefcase and hurriedly kissed her Mistress goodbye. "I'll try to call this afternoon, I love you."

"Love you too."

They hugged and clung to each other like saran wrap for a few seconds.

Carmen went back to the kitchen for more coffee. She was restless. Something felt off. She wouldn't go so far as to say Lo chose baby puke over having intimacy with her, but in a way, isn't that what just happened? She brooded.

She should've ordered Lo to take the day off. She checked the calendar. They hadn't played in almost seven weeks. Unreal! How did that even happen? Was Lo withdrawing? She wasn't acting differently except when it came to playtime. Lo had a different excuse every time. Either she was too tired, had too much paperwork, or had a headache; it was always something. Was she avoiding play? The lack of kink in their lives was getting to Carmen.

Once Lo left, Carmen idly opened a porn site and slipped her hand into her sweatpants. It felt as if she'd seen all the good porn already. All she could find now seemed so uninspired. Or maybe it was just too early in the day for porn. Porn was better at night, especially on nights when Lo fell asleep on the couch.

She shut her laptop and went to the bathroom to get ready for work. She had an appointment that afternoon with a new client, the wife of an art collector who, the dossier reported, had amassed a fortune in art and hid it all in a room the wife had never been allowed to enter. Strange, but the kind of strange hoarding she'd become accustomed to with the super wealthy. They'd pay millions for something only to lock it away, never to be seen by anyone else ever again. At least until they died and their heirs called in people like her.

Carmen stared into the mirror and saw an older version of herself looking back. She perennially felt like she was in her 20s but her face looked every bit of her 50 years. Her mother's people were from the Volta region of Ghana and Carmen inherited their light brown skin and wide, slim lips, while her white Jewish father bestowed upon her all his wrinkles and his hooked nose. She was too proud to consider plastic surgery for her nose or Botox for her forehead, but it bothered her at times when people mistook her for Lo's mother. Lo, at age 48, still got carded at wine stores and clubs, which was alternately hilarious and annoying to Carmen. Lo's parents were Haitian refugees, and their daughter's skin was seemingly untouched by time. The only change she saw in Lo was that her breasts hung lower and her hips were wider than when they met. Carmen, on the other hand, was still thin as a reed. Instead of getting rounder with age, she was getting flatter. She sighed. You can fight the world, but you can't fight your genes.

She focused on her task. Her project for the day was to help the rich socialite get her dead husband's collection ready for auction. Her project manager at Sotheby's said it wouldn't take too long, as he'd already researched the collector's history and by his estimation, there were only a handful of pieces that were worth putting on the block. On the other hand, that handful could sell for very high prices, so he asked that Carmen look for specific pieces and call him when they were all found. The fun of it, for her, was when she found good stuff that the guy didn't know about, and then called her gallery contacts to broker private sales. There was a lot more profit in being an agent than a consultant.

Carmen got another cup of coffee and then got to work. After making lists, she called the moving crew, confirmed the schedule, and called a few business contacts to see who was hungry for new work. The art market died during the worst of COVID but was finally seeing a little movement again. She glanced at her iPhone -- she still had an hour to kill before the appointment with the late-collector's wife.

She dialed the number she always called at times like this.

"Jax's World of Weirdness!" a cheery voice greeted her. "How may we warp you today?"

"Corey, is Jax free?"

"Hello, Carmen! See, I knew it was you! I'm psychic."

"Don't you have caller ID?"

"Well, geee, okay, be that way."

"I mean, you aren't greeting marketers like that, are you?"

"And what if I were?" he said.

"Damn, Corey." She laughed.

"The Commander is commanding me to surrender her phone."

Carmen heard Jax in the background. "That's enough," Jax was saying to him. She grabbed her phone.

"Bye-ee, Carmen," he cried in the distance.

"Carmen, darling, hello, hello," Jax said.

"OMG, Corey. No," Carmen replied.

"Right?" Jax said. "So cheerful in the morning I could kill him."

"How can you live with all the dad jokes?"

"I blame the kids," Jax said. "He is in full-on dad mode and can't stop."

"Or maybe he's happy you got back from Denver."

"Maybe. Yeah, he is." Jax's voice softened.

* * *

From the day they first met, the two women felt a sisterly bond that could not be explained. Maybe it was humor. Maybe it was that instant recognition kinksters had of those who shared their predilections. Kink was funny that way. You met a kinky stranger from another world, another life, another culture, and within an hour you knew them in ways no one else ever had.

For Jax, meeting Carmen would always be linked to her love of Grandpa Paul. Carmen was assigned to curate Paul's art when Jax was clearing out his house. She remembered when Carmen stepped inside of an extra room, feet away from Jax's old bedroom, and gasped with pleasure. "I've never seen so many dicks in one place before! Was he gay?" she asked.

"Queer as a pink dollar bill," Jax sang out.

"You sound proud of it," Carmen said cautiously.

"I am proud of it!" Jax said. "Best man I've ever known. A brilliant artist too. You'll see. By the way, I identify as queer myself." They both froze. Jax wondered if the art appraiser would turn homophobic on her while Carmen wondered if she should admit she was lesbian. Both decided to stick to business.

"Excuse me," Carmen said, grabbing her work uniform. It all looked very clean, but she still wasn't going to risk touching a cockroach or finding rat turds behind the heaps of art.

"We might have a couple of things in common," Carmen said, breaking the silence.

"I knew I liked you," Jax answered.

"You seem like good people."

"You too." They shared a long look.

"Well, then, that's settled," Carmen said, and Jax laughed.

"I guess we're friends now!"

"Could be," Carmen said. Then she paused. "Possibly kinky?"

"VERY kinky! SO kinky!"

Carmen held up her palm and they high-fived. Jax cried, "Woof!" Carmen woofed back, and their friendship was set in stone.

Paul was the most prolific artist Carmen had yet encountered. There were unfinished paintings and many that weren't quite museum gallery quality, but she was already lining up smaller galleries in her mind that would be happy to have them. She also found treasures she knew the auction house would take.

She relied on Jax to help sort the work by decade and into periods. Collectors loved knowing all the trivia on when and where and why artists made their work.

"I first saw this one when I was around seven," Jax said as she held up a large canvas.

"Very progressive parents."

"Hardly! My father, who was his son, took me there in secret. I thought they were gummy worms."

Carmen hooted. "At that age, yeah, I guess so."

"I thought my father's friend was just a friend, too," Jax added.

"Oof! He brought his girlfriend?"

"Boyfriend."

"Hoooo-ho! So that's how it was."

"Here are Paul's reviews." Jax opened a scrapbook of faded clips that she had arranged by date. "I typed up a chronological list of all the galleries that showed his work." She turned to the back of the scrapbook where a list was tucked into a pocket of the back cover.

"Impressive!"

Carmen was as pleased by the granddaughter's devotion as she was by the rave reviews from art critics. Until then, she'd never heard of Paul. When she first saw all the penis paintings, she didn't think they'd have much commercial value. Reading the reviews gave her hope. She recognized some esteemed critics among them, and they described him as a pioneer of gay abstract expressionism. Now she saw his work through a queer lens. His talent was very obvious, even if his subject was redundant. "This is wonderful," Carmen said after looking through the scrapbook. "It gives credibility and historic value to his estate. I bet someone will want to buy the scrapbook too."

"The price isn't as important as people loving it and wanting to hang the work in their homes," Jax said. "I know that's what Paul would want.

"Prices are how we know how much they love it in this business," Carmen said.

"Ah," Jax said. "I guess we'll find out how much they care, then."

The next time they met was a few months later, at the auction uptown. They waved across the room and hugged each other hard. Between their first meeting and the auction, they had spent so much time on Zoom together, they had become really close. They talked about art first. Jax told her everything about Paul the artist and Paul the man. Carmen told her about Lo, then Jax told her about Corey. Then they talked about BDSM, their philosophies of kink, and compared their experience as lifestyle Femdoms. Jax revealed she had been a Pro-Domme for 20 years; Carmen admitted she dipped her toes into Pro-Domming when art jobs were lean.

On the day of the auction, Carmen's boss presented a PowerPoint of the reviews, mixed with photos of Paul in his studio. The rich history of his career drove bidders wild. Half of them probably didn't know who Paul was when they walked into the room that day, but the PowerPoint presentation created visible excitement. The auction turned out better than expected, pulling in prices that got a headline in ARTnews.

The huge success of the auction experience brought them even closer. Jax said it gave her closure to know his legacy would live on. Carmen got a letter from the auction house praising her creative staging of the art and included a bonus for exceeding their sales expectations. Even the scrapbook sold for a big price.

That night, they went out for a celebratory dinner and drank a lot of wine. Carmen insisted on paying, and said, "You can treat me next time."

Jax bit her lip. "There will be a next time, right?"

"Of course," Carmen said. "I'm not giving you up!"

"I can't give you up!" Jax said. "I've never felt this close to another dominant woman, and I don't want to let go of what we have."

"Me neither."

Jax paused. "Let's start a family."

"What?" Carmen set down her wineglass. "I can't have kids with you!" She smiled.

"No, I mean, let's start a Leather Family together. No, really, we should. I already know half a dozen people to invite to join us. Wouldn't that be wonderful? To have our own special family."

"I'll have to discuss it with Lo," Carmen said. She liked the idea. But Lo, always afraid of being outed for work reasons, might not.

"See? That's where we're different. I'm just going to tell

Corey."

Carmen laughed. "Well, men are more malleable..."

"OK, now I know for sure you are lesbian," Jax said.

"If we call it anything, let's call it Jax's Family," Carmen said.

"Oh no, that's too weird."

"Honey, I don't have a soul other than Lo to invite! So it'll be your friends, your invitations, and besides, it's your idea. I think that's the way to go. It also sounds better if it's Jax's Family rather than, I don't know, Clan of the Kinky Cave Bear or some other ridiculous name."

"It sounds like a hospice service, but okay." Jax drained her glass, and the rest was history.

It worked out well for all. Lo was charmed by the idea, Corey was enthusiastic, and soon Marco and Gigi joined their Zoom meetings so Carmen could get to know them. A few years later, Mariangela joined, and they decided to stop there because once you added in everyone's partners, it was just the right number of people to play in their New York apartments without drawing too much attention to themselves. Except for Gigi and her gang, who were always traveling, Jax's Family, such as it was, met at each other's homes once a month for play parties and began meeting up for coffee or dinner on weekends too. Marco and Corey went out together to cigar bars, while his boys occasionally kidnapped Corey to play video games with them. Carmen and Jax went on shopping sprees together. When Mariangela was available, she joined the Femdoms for their weekly brunches. Lo regularly sat for Corey, who couldn't make enough sketches of her face and physique, but Lo's favorite time was spent with the kids, who called her Auntie and begged for her to tell them stories. It had all worked out better than Carmen ever expected. Now they had a formalized network of people they could count on, with Jax at the head.

"So how's Jax's Family doing?" Carmen asked.

"Kids are good," Jax said.

"No, I meant your adult children," Carmen said. "How's the Denver contingent?"

"Everything is stable in Gigi's world right now. No one's sick, they love their house, and the youngers are such a blessing."

"Oh good. Gigi's fatigue okay?"

"About the same. She gets tired a lot. Her back and right arm are not aging well."

"I wonder if anyone ever studied how many whip strokes you can give before your back and shoulder go to hell. Shouldn't we know that?"

"Right? Like maybe doctors should offer Whip-Arm Rehab to people like us."

"Can you imagine a roomful of Femdoms waiting to see the doctor, kvetching about how whipping ruined their lives?"

"Yeah! Damn those masochists and their greedy way of forcing us to hurt them."

They both snickered. Humor was their golden pass to eternal friendship. Though they agreed that Corey was hilarious in a disconcertingly corny way, their mutual senses of humor were perfectly complementary.

"And Marco?"

"He's really settled into his new life in Denver. He's making a killing at real estate. I don't think he'll ever come back to New York except for visits to see us."

"Wow, he likes it that much?"

"He likes it so much he almost sold me on buying a house out there myself."

"Really! You think you're ready to leave New York?"

"Yes and no. Yes, I'm ready for a better life for the kids and Corey, and no, you're here, and so are all my memories."

"I'd visit you!"

"I know but it wouldn't be the same. Still, okay, I confess, I did look at a couple of places with him."

"Aha!" Carmen said. "I knew it!"

"You did?" Jax was surprised. She herself hadn't agreed to look at homes until Marco whisked her away one day to see how much better her family could live out there for much less than she paid in New York.

"Alright, Marco told me he showed you homes," Carmen said. "I just wanted to see if you'd tell me."

"Bitch."

"Real estate slut."

"We'll see, we'll see. But you'll have to move there too."

"You know, there's art everywhere," Carmen said. "New York's getting to be too much for me and Lo. She won't admit it, but, my God, her workload has doubled since COVID. She acts like it doesn't bother her, but I can almost taste the burnout. You know, we haven't played in seven weeks???"

"What? I didn't realize the dry spell had lasted that long. Oooh. Not great. So what's up with you and Lo?" Jax asked. "Any happy time lately? Play?"

"No, Jax, it is not great at all," Carmen said. "Today she ditched me for the baby who barfed on her tits."

"Oh God, I remember when that happened! EUW. I'm sorry you're in a rut with your wife. It happens, I know, but it sucks."

"I mean, okay, I understand that work stresses her out. So she doesn't feel the mood much. But you and I both know it's a slippery slope when your sub stops wanting you."

"I know," Jax said. "It's been pretty iffy with Corey, too."

"The thing is, how do you get a sub out of that place without just ordering it and then risking blow-back afterward? Like today, I could tell it irritated her that I was trying to get her to stay home. I remember when she loved to be ordered to take days off."

"Oh, yeah, I'm sorry. It's even worse when you think they're just doing it for you, not because they're hot for it."

"That's it, exactly. I don't want to nag her. I want her to want it. You can't Dom someone into wanting something they don't want. That's hideous."

"Yeah, you're right, they have to want it for their own reasons."

They said, "Hmm!" at the same time.

"Maybe set up a kinky date for weekends? Tell her to shave, maybe cook dinner for you in the nude. A long prep could put her in the mood. Make her focus on serving, so she can stew in subbie juices for a while?"

"I could do that. It could maybe work. Worst case, I get her famous beef and pumpkin soup!"

"Oh my God, I love that dish!"

"OK, I'm going to wait until Friday. She thinks I'm going out of town, but I'm going to cancel the trip and surprise her when she gets home."

"How cute. Nice way to start!"

"I'll go into Bitch-Domme mode and order her around. I'll tell her I expect fresh, smooth pussy and a sparkling clean ass."

"Inspect them."

"Yes, I will, I'll scrutinize her labia and butt like they were works of art. Which they are, in my opinion."

"With a flashlight and magnifier?"

"With a flashlight and magnifier, good thinking! I won't be tender about it, either. I'll treat her like a piece of meat."

"Classic move! And after that?"

"Well, you know, I'm going to draw it out, spend a lot of time teasing her. I won't stop until she is gushing. How about tushie play? Too soon?"

"What?! Never too soon! You can't NOT do tushie play."

"Right? Ass play is the new oral. No heavy whips, though. Take her along slowly."

"Agreed. More sensual swoons than screams."

"Exactly. In fact, I'm getting the Sybian out of the toy closet. Gonna re-sanitize it and lube it up nice. It will glisten."

"Lucky Lo," Jax whistled.

"She's going to ride that pony until she can't, then I'll peel her off and carry her to bed."

"Aww, that's romantic."

"Also necessary. Her legs won't work by the time she's done riding."

Jax roared. "Hawt!"

"You know Gigi's little ritual of making her slaves repeat their vows every night?"

"Of course. I love it. It's adorable."

"I should do that. Make her be fully present in her submission every day. Maybe twice a day. Or would that be too much? Some nights she brings home paperwork. Which reminds me, guess what, she's in line for a promotion!"

"Congratulations!!! You guys are rocking it!"

"She'll be rocking the Sybian this weekend."

"Ha! As for the vow thing, maybe once a day? She's pretty stressed out in the mornings, right?"

"Yeah she is, but... I don't know. I'm really missing my 24/7 horny slavey-girl, you know?"

"Well, okay, but if she wakes up with work energy, she might resent you trying to push her into subspace. Way different energies. But, I don't know, I'm just thinking out loud."

"No, it's a valid point," Carmen said. "Anyhoo... so, yeah, I'm getting us back to where we should be! I just need that feeling, you know? The high."

"Totally get it," Jax replied. "Same here. Can't go too long without or I don't feel like myself. Fortunately, Corey is a kink-hungry beast, so he's always begging for it."

"That's right, girl, flaunt it," Carmen said drily.

"Not flaunting, just, you know," Jax hesitated, "bragging!"

They giggled together.

"OK, so you got this, Carmen. Oh, wait, she has a praise kink, right? Give her lots of that this weekend."

"Ooh, yeah, thanks, Jax. It's good to bounce ideas off you. You're the best." Carmen checked the time. "Well, I gotta head out now. Moving a collection this afternoon."

"Nice! I won't keep you. I love you to the moon."

"Wait! How are you feeling?"

"OK."

"Continue."

"Ok, but cramping a lot."

"Any new symptoms?"

"Nah. Probably a passing thing. I'll be okay. And, seriously, you need to get to work so let's end."

"OK," Carmen said. "But you'll tell me if something changes?"

"Of course," Jax said. "Who else am I going to whine to?"

"I love you to Venus!" Carmen said.

"I love you to Uranus!" It was their own twisted little goodbye ritual.

They hung up and Carmen smiled at her phone. Jax was the best friend she'd ever had. She was so kind, so funny, and an invaluable source of kink wisdom.

Carmen imagined Lo's face when she saw Mistress was still home and the Sybian was set up. That would be a moment! And, if it went as she believed it would, the moment would last all weekend.

She knew she was starting to run late for her appointment, but she lingered at her desk anyway, gazing at a framed photo of their wedding day. Younger Lo's face was radiant with worshipful love. Younger Carmen was calm, confident, and proud as any Femdom would be to own such a sweet, beautiful woman. The photo captured their internal realities. Proud Mistress and happy slave. That's who they were born to be. It's who they had to be. If she succeeded at nothing else, Carmen was going to succeed at re-awakening her wife's slave heart.

Chapter 8

WE EVOLVE TOGETHER

Just when life seems to hold no more surprises, just when you are set in your ways and damn proud of it, a new reality throws you out of your comfort zone. Can you change? You don't want to. But will you change? Yes. Even if the change you make is to fight change, you will change. The real question is whether you possess the courage to adapt to change.

"Welcome to Torture-Land, where all the sluts cum!" She held up her weapon: an old-fashioned, plug-in vibrator that Leon hard-wired to the wall. She held it over Milli's face and buzzed her nose.

"Boop," she said. "I booped your nose."

"Staaaap," Milli pretend-slapped it away like it was a fly.

"Boop!" Gigi said. "Now I booped your nipple!"

"Arghhhh!" Milli said. "Nooooo."

"Aha," Gigi said as she pressed the soft plump head between Milli's legs.

Milli sighed and shuddered.

"Looks like I booped the right spot!"

"Yes, Ma'am... Oh yes."

Milli writhed as Gigi slowly massaged her crotch, teasing her.

"Why are there pants? Did I tell you to wear pants?"

"Oh no, Ma'am, you didn't, but..."

"Did I give you permission to wear them?"

"No, Ma'am, no you did not."

The two women paused to smile at each other. "I love you, Ma'am."

"I love you too, in my own cold-hearted way," Gigi winked.

The day hadn't begun well. Gigi went to bed last night with an agonizing migraine and woke up still feeling pain in her eyes. The smallest sound irritated her. The grinding of coffee beans, the clatter of a spoon stirring a cup, every sound triggered a small hurricane in her skull. The pill was bringing her back to life as the migraine softened and retreated. She was so grateful for that until she realized her stomach was growling and churning. It felt like gut demons were dancing around in her intestines, making her twitch with pain where they collided.

When Milli brought Ma'am her morning coffee, she was concerned that Gigi was still in bed.

"Good morning, Ma'am, are you feeling any better?"

"The migraine is finally gone." She took the coffee cup and gulped it. She had places to go today and people to spank.

"Oh good!" Milli sighed. "I really missed our play-time last night."

"Oh, did you?" Gigi said. "I never would have guessed from the way you curled up in a ball of self-pity that you didn't get your weekend spanking on time."

"Oh, Ma'am, I was just sorry you felt so bad."

"Uh-huh." Gigi knew better. At 71, Milli still acted like the greedy, giggly slut she'd always been.

"Really! I'm so happy you are feeling good."

"Well, don't get too cheerful," Gigi said, "because my guts feel like someone's tap dancing in there."

"Oh nooooooo!" Milli gasped. "Are you okay? Do you want me to call the doctor?"

"Oh, goodness no, my sweet, it's probably gas fighting its way through my flipping intestines. I'll feel better when I fart."

"So will I," Milli giggled.

"Stop that, you little piggy. Get your mind out of my ass." Milli rolled with laughter. "I will never understand how a well-raised woman like you is so excited by body odors."

"Oink, oink!" Milli said. Gigi tickled her belly and made her slave girl nearly hysterical.

"I shouldn't have had so much coffee last night."

"Or wine?"

"Or wine. Or pot."

"Maybe it was the Mexican food."

"There's that, but Jesus, I'm not giving up tacos!" The food memory made her nauseous and she belched loudly, tasting decayed beans. "Well, that's a start, I guess. One way or another, it's going to be a gassy day."

Gigi always thought getting old meant you got more tired and needed more sleep, or got some horrendous disease and died. Now she realized that, no, seniority was a tiresome long crawl through decay. One day it was a swollen knee, the next day it was a sore wrist, then a small bone that broke for no reason, and when that healed, hello constipation, fuck you arthritis, and eat shit and die UTIs. It was a constant merry-go-round of painful events that forced you to carry an awareness of mortal fragility you never felt before. Now she understood why old people got tired and needed more sleep: half their lives were about healing from the stress of streaming indignities.

"Are you sure that's all it is?" Milli asked as she sat down beside her and leaned in for her morning kiss.

"I'm sure that I'd like a distraction." Gigi narrowed her eyes. She couldn't turn back the clock, so she would move it forward by focusing on fun. "You're always a good distraction."

Milli automatically fell backward on the bed, tummy up. Gigi idly stroked her face, playing with her nostrils while Milli pretend-protested, "Not my nostrils!"

"Well, if I can't torture your nostrils," Gigi pretend-huffed, "I guess I'll have to torture you elsewhere."

The doorbell rang. The women looked at each other in shock.

"Who dares to ring Mistress Gigi's doorbell?!" they said at the same time.

"Oh my God, you're turning into me," said Gigi.

"Oh my God, I wish," Milli said as she zipped her pants back up. "Should I answer?"

"No, stay with me. Leon will get it."

A loud fart filled the air, audibly and fragrantly.

"Mmmmmm," Milli giggled again.

"There, I've blessed the visitor at the door," Gigi said calmly. "They may leave now."

Milli was delighted. "May Fortune smell on them!"

Then the doorbell rang again. And again. It kept on ringing until at last, they heard Leon run down the stairs. They heard him open the door and converse with someone, but they couldn't make out what either party said.

"Maybe it's a package delivery," Milli said.

"At this hour? Not unless they FedExed it to us."

"Maybe Jax sent something?"

"She'd tell me first if she did. She knows I don't like surprises."

Leon climbed back up the stairs and stood in the doorway looking perplexed.

"There's a kid at the door. She says she wants to come in and meet us." He scratched his head. "I don't know, but she seems like a nice kid."

"Are you kidding?" Milli said.

"I wouldn't kid about a kid," Leon said.

"Shut up, you two, oh my God. How old is this kid, Leon? You know the only children we allow in here are Miranda and Zane and always under supervision."

"Oh, she's not that young, I'd say in her late 20s, maybe."

Gigi's stomach started talking so loudly she wondered if the others could hear it. *Borborygmi* is what the doctor called it. Normal, he said. But it didn't feel normal to her. She farted again.

"Give me five minutes, I better hit the john."

"What about the kid?"

"Leave her outside! I will deal with this when I'm done."

Leon went back downstairs to tell the girl that the Mistress of the House would be there shortly to speak with her. The girl almost fell over when he used those words. Leon assumed she was just a klutz and closed the door on her apologetically.

When he got upstairs, Gigi was coming out of the bathroom and wearing a blouse, pants, and lipstick. "You look good!" he said heartily.

"I'm feeling a lot better. Now who is this person and why is she here?"

"She says she's a neighbor and she looked us up on the Internet," he reported. "She wants to get to know us."

Milli looked horrified. "Oh, no, an Internet stalker! I don't like this, I don't like this at all."

Milli put her hands over her ears and paced. "La, la, la, it's not happening, la, la."

Leon couldn't resist. "They're coming to take you away, ha-ha! They're coming to take you away," he sang.

"Hell no, I won't go!" Milli chimed back.

"You two," Gigi said as she pointed at them, "get your asses out of the 1960s and sit and stew in the moment. Milli stop catastrophizing. She could be a Jehovah's Witness."

"AGHHHHH!!!!" Milli cried.

Leon shook his head. "She won't wanna witness what goes on here."

Their penchant for speaking in puns was hellacious, yet endlessly amusing. She gave them stern looks and went downstairs to banish the visitor.

She peered through the Judas Eye and saw a young woman in a black sleeveless dress, arms and legs covered in tattoos. Above the neck, she had nose rings and earrings, and her hair was dyed black. Gigi thought she saw a Triskele on one arm but dismissed it. Kids today didn't even know what some of the symbols they stamped on their skin really meant. If it looked cool, they added it to their collection. She remembered when tattoos really meant something. When they were sacred. What did a slice of pizza on someone's bicep even mean?

"May I help you?" Gigi said graciously, opening the door to her.

The girl made a weird movement that resembled a curtsy.

"I'm sorry to bother you, Ma'am, I'm sure you like your privacy."

"I do," Gigi said curtly. She assessed her cunningly. The girl wasn't doing door-to-door sales, she wasn't carrying anything. She wasn't taking a poll or registering voters, she didn't have a pad and pen. And definitely not a religious nut with all those body modifications. Although she heard that, these days, you can be inked up and down and still find a church that would take you. "What do you want?"

"So, I'm living with my Aunt Emily right now because she's sick. She has a nurse, but she needed someone to take care of her dogs, and my mother couldn't come because she teaches and she'd lose her tenure if she left, and my father travels all the time. He's never around, so he couldn't do it, plus my sister is nine months pregnant and our younger brother is an asshole, so that left me, and so here I am. It sucks worse than I expected!" The young woman was talking so fast that Gigi thought she might have mental problems.

"Christ, kid, I could die at any minute. Get to the point," Gigi said.

"I'm from Michigan and I don't know anybody here and everybody here is so straight." Then she whispered. "Aunt Emily is MAGA. It's so hard to live with her, but there's no one else to care for her dogs and before she moved here, I played with them every day, so they're almost like my dogs. I can't let them go to a shelter and my parents won't let me bring them back to Michigan. Please, please could I visit you? I'm helpful, I can clean and do laundry for you. I can do any chores you want. I won't be a burden, I promise."

"Visit? You mean come inside our home? No."

Rule Number One of Gigi's House was that strangers were not allowed. Everyone who entered had to be vetted for their values and discretion. It was different at Marco's place in the hip part of the city. People there were friendly and open-minded. He could invite fresh meat in full leather without fear. But around here, if neighbors had the slightest suspicion something was too liberated for their small brains to fathom, they'd grab their pitchforks and guns.

The girl looked so crushed that Gigi felt shitty about turning her away. The kid had to be lonely living here, but it was on her to find more suitable friends. "I'm sorry, but we are old folk, and there's nothing here for you."

"Oh, I'm sure that's not true," the girl said. "I'm sure there is so much I could learn from you just by hanging out."

Gigi inhaled sharply. "Hanging out? With us?" The old woman cackled. "What would we do together? Play Scrabble?"

"I like Scrabble." The girl smiled. "But I did a lot of Googling to find out your deadname, and then I read about you on a BDSM history website. I even saw pictures of you when you were Mistress Lucinda. I hope it's okay to say that."

Gigi's spine stiffened with paranoia. So this sneaky little bitch had tracked her down on the Internet. Milli was right. She was a stalker! Or maybe she thought they'd give her money if she threatened to out them. This child had no idea what Gigi had been through -- the threats, the arrests, the harassment. Oh no, this time, Gigi was going to fight back. She would report the kid as a vandal, a stalker, a blackmailer.

The girl searched the old woman's face and got nervous. "I'm sorry, I always say too much." What I really wanted to tell you is that I felt so much joy when I found you, like finally there were people I could talk to." She glanced around nervously and lowered her voice. "I am one of you."

Gigi was still plotting how to fight this kid to the death. "You're what? Speak up."

The girl looked afraid. "I'm one of you," she said meekly. "I'm kinky." She pointed to the Triskele tattoo on her right arm. "You know what that is, right? It's so lonely for me here." Her eyes got misty. "You're one of my heroes now. It's so sacred to me that you live just a few doors away from my aunt. Like we were destined to meet."

Gigi wasn't entirely sure she bought it, but decided to give her the benefit of the doubt. "What's your name, kinky girl?"

"My Scene name is Sassy Lassie."

"Your real name."

"Marla. Marla Culberson. I'm staying with my aunt, Emily Culberson. Do you know her?"

"Is she the one with the wheelchair and Corgis?"

"Yes! That's why I came here, so I could take care of them."

"Won't she get curious if you visit us?"

"Oh no, not Aunt Emily, she isn't curious about anything, especially not about me. I don't even stay in the main house. I live in the shed out back." Marla shook her head. "The nurse won't even let me see her unless my arms and legs are covered. She says Aunt Em gets upset when she sees my tattoos because she thinks they are signs of the devil."

"The storage shed?" Gigi gasped.

"Well, I cleaned it out and fixed it up, it's more like a tiny home now. I like it."

Gigi looked her over again. Leon was wrong: Marla was young, but not too young, closer to 30 than to 20.

"You do know we're all over 70 in this house, right?"

"Age doesn't matter!" Marla said. "You dress cool, not like the pastels and plaids crowd around here. And you go to the queer-owned shops."

"We do?" Gigi feigned surprise. Of course, they knew they were patronizing the LGBT-owned businesses, they had rainbow stickers all over their windows and doors, for Christ's sake. That's exactly why they chose to do business there.

"I've seen you eating at Lavender Spice and buying plants at The Thistle. They're both owned by gay people."

"You don't say."

Marla shot Gigi a knowing look. "I bet you voted for Biden!"

"You're damn right we did," Gigi said.

"See? You're not really..." Marla trailed off.

"Old?" Gigi said. "Irrelevant? Demented?"

"Boomers," Marla said. "You're old but you don't act like old people."

Gigi was nonplussed. Her take on Marla was that she was a sweet but very confused young woman if she was trying to hook up with senior citizens at her young age. "Marla, don't take this the wrong way, you seem like a lovely person, but, really, it's not a good idea. We're in such a different stage of life. You should be out having fun at clubs and dating... the gender of your choice."

"Oh, please." Marla rolled her eyes. "The dating scene around here is pathetic. Besides, you are a goddess to me, a real-life hero! Like an OG sex revolutionary."

The old woman's eyes narrowed. Was she trying to convince her with flattery, because it was working! It wasn't every day that a stranger called her a goddess. It made her heart stir a little.

"What does OG mean?"

"Original generation."

Gigi didn't understand what that meant but a random gas pain made her indifferent to kid slang. She grimaced. This made Marla jitter.

"I hope I didn't hurt your feelings." Marla folded her hands together beseechingly. "Please, at least give me a chance to meet you all." She sank to her knees in front of the old woman. "Pleeeeeease?"

"Oh for Christ's sake, get off your knees, what are you thinking, a neighbor could see."

Maybe she could bend her rules this one time, Gigi thought. Whatever her precise age, Marla was older now than Gigi was when she married the bum who left her for a stripper.

"Go on, go inside." She opened the door wide. "Jesus, Joseph and Mary, what's wrong with young people, just getting on your knees in the cold light of day, have you all gone crazy?"

Marla jumped to her feet and tried to hug Gigi.

"That's a hard no," Gigi pushed her away.

Marla shrank back. "I understand, Ma'am, I'm sorry. I didn't mean to disrespect you."

"Just get in here, before someone sees you." The old woman checked the street. It was quiet as ever, not a pitchfork in sight.

She led Marla to the kitchen and called up to her bedroom. "Milli! Leon! Get down here now! RIGHT NOW!"

"Come on," she said to Marla, "you can sit with us for a few minutes but I'm telling you, this isn't going anywhere, okay?"

"Really?! Thank you! Thank you so much!" Marla looked like she just joined the circus. She scampered to the kitchen table and plopped into a seat like she was already part of the sideshow.

Leon and Milli rushed in excitedly then froze when they saw a young person at the table.

"We're all going to sit down and have a little talk," Gigi said. "Milli and Leon, meet Marla. Marla, meet Milli and Leon." She looked around the table. "Leon, Milli, Marla wants to hang out with us."

"Hang out???" Milli hooted. "What are you, 22?"

"I'm 33," Marla said. "I'm not young."

"You're not young at 33?" Leon was amused. "I'm old enough to be your grandfather."

"OK," Marla shrugged, "I care about who people are, not their age."

The elders hushed with embarrassment. Of course, they hated agism, and of course, they resented when younger people treated them as irrelevant antiques who were gobbling up resources that properly belonged to the young. But they hated it at a distance. Up close, they avoided young people. Now, they felt like hypocrites for judging her by her age.

"Marla, tell us how you found us," Gigi broke the silence.

"Oh, yeah, of course. So, I saw you on NextDoor, and then I saw you going to cool places in your cool clothes, and I just knew there had to be a story there. I Googled you but I couldn't find anything, so I tried image searches. It took days and a lot of different keywords but finally, I was able to match your avatar to some old photos of a woman called Lucinda March."

Marla looked triumphant, but Milli looked sick at the revelation.

"After that, I uncovered a trove of Mistress Lucinda memorabilia. You were so beautiful, such a goddess. I didn't understand why I'd never heard about you, but eventually, I found some articles about your legal problems and how you vanished mysteriously into thin air! Then I got it. You were a renegade in your youth! So cool!"

Milli was nervously rapping her fingers on the table. Leon leaned back in his chair and closed his eyes, his face stoic. This was their nightmare come true. Whether or not warrants had expired, whether or not anyone was alive to care, the fear was still there, the fear that their precious Gigi would be publicly humiliated or put on trial for crimes that weren't even crimes, and, worst of all, that she would be taken from them.

"How did you find the first picture? Leon, please tell me you didn't upload Ma'am's face to social media?!" Milli cried.

"Well..." he fumbled, "I didn't think anyone... I didn't know about image searches and..."

"Oh fuck," Gigi sighed. "Are you fucking kidding me, Leon?"

"Mistress, I am beside myself with self-loathing..."

"How many times did I tell you not to open an account for me on social media," Gigi said with quiet rage. "This is all your fault.

Milli turned on him too. "Why loathe yourself when we can do that for you!"

"I'm so, so sorry." Leon hung his head. "I didn't see the harm. Now I do. I'll delete them right away." He got on his phone and took care of it. "Done!"

"God only knows who else has connected the kinky dots," Gigi said.

"Oh, I doubt anyone has," Marla piped up. "I mean, it took me weeks to put it all together, and I'm a hacker!"

They looked at her incredulously. "Isn't hacking illegal?" Leon asked.

"Oh, I don't do malicious hacking. I'm just saying I'm very good at digging stuff out of the Internet, and really good with the Way Back Machine."

"See, Milli?" Leon tried to be jovial. "Marla goes all the way back!"

Milli didn't smile, she was still too disgusted to look at him.

"And what's this about a trove of memorabilia?"

"I found it on a BDSM history site. It said someone named Master Michael donated the pictures. Do you know him?"

"Not a clue," they all said. But they did know a submissive named Michael who had stalked Gigi for years, sending letters to her abroad to prove to them and himself that he knew who they were. Motherfucking slave Michael. Did he become a top later in life? What a joke.

The elders signaled each other with their eyes. Milli was dubious. Leon was curious. Gigi didn't know how she felt about the girl.

Marla was forthcoming and honest, maybe a little too honest, but Gigi appreciated her transparency. She was kind of cute, too, with her goth fashion sense and earnest manner. Anyone who'd pick up their lives and move to another state to save dogs from the pound was a good person in her book. That took a kind heart, courage, and commitment. It was a shame to see her trapped by circumstances.

Gigi briefly met the kid's aunt the first week they moved in. She was in a wheelchair with Corgis tied to a rail, and a uniformed nurse pushing. She made a fuss about stopping in front of Gigi's house and tried to peek through their windows with binoculars.

"Oh fuck, what the hell!" Gigi had immediately stormed outside to stare her down. "Can I help you?" she shouted.

"I'm Mrs. Culberson." The woman in the chair had said her name as if Gigi would be impressed. Gigi wasn't. The woman looked insulted and ordered her nurse to take her home immediately. Gigi never saw her again. She was a bitch through and through to make her niece sleep in her garden shed when she owned the biggest house on the block, maybe 8,000 square feet or more. The kid could have had an entire wing to herself without disturbing the aunt. It reminded her of her own miserable fucking aunt, the one who reneged on the furniture and cut her off when she learned how Gigi made her living. Gigi knew what it was like to be judged by your own blood.

She felt her sympathy rising.

Marla pleaded softly, "I'm not asking you to do anything but talk sometimes, or you don't even have to talk, I'd learn just by being in your presence. I know you don't need me, but I promise I'll be the best service sub. Please. I have a slave heart," she said. "I'm afraid if I don't use it, it'll wither and die."

The elders shifted uncomfortably in their chairs. They remembered what it felt like to live alone with your kinks, not knowing if or when you'd find someone who would understand. They understood the loneliness and despair of it. The trio exchanged glances, speaking with their eyes to each other. They couldn't abandon a kinky person to the hell of straight judgment, to a woman who thought Marla was marked by the devil. What kind of bullshit was that?

Gigi leaned back. She'd decided. Marla was okay. A service sub was always a wonderful addition to a Leather Household. It probably wouldn't go anywhere, but it would be nice while it lasted to see a young face around, especially if she could do some of the chores they were too old to deal with. She would be perfect to help care for their grumpy old dogs. That would really help. The dogs were already making nice with her, putting their shaggy heads in Marla's lap and wagging their tails when she petted them.

"Leon, make us all some brunch. Marla will eat with us."

"Yes, Ma'am!" He jumped to his feet.

"Ma'am," Marla asked shyly, "are Leon and Milli your submissives?"

"Slaves," Gigi said sharply.

"We've been serving Mistress for 39 years. Our 40th anniversary is in January."

Marla clasped her hands in joy. "Oh, thank God, I've found you. I am so grateful, so grateful, thank you for allowing me to get to know you."

"We'll expect you here at least one day a week," Gigi said.

"Just one? I can do more."

"Then we'll expect you here at least more days a week." Gigi smiled at her.

"That's wonderful! Thank you, Ma'am!"

Now an all-new chapter of their lives began. A chapter that included Marla. Gigi, of course, made new rules and boundaries. The elders spent days discussing how to protect her by not getting too dependent on her service so she could leave them as soon as she met people her own age. They wouldn't let her get too attached to them either. It wouldn't be fair to her.

Naturally, within a few weeks, Marla had burrowed into their hearts. Her cheerful attitude and optimism lifted them up. She was great with their dogs and very conscientious about her duties. Wherever they went, Marla was always available to lend a hand. She weeded alongside Leon, and helped Milli in the kitchen, gathering ingredients and lifting heavy trays out of the oven for her. In Denver, Marla had worked as a licensed masseuse. Her deep tissue massages were so effective, Gigi became more mobile, and her neck didn't crackle and pop anymore. There was no other way to see it but as a blessing to have Marla in their lives.

Marla was exactly as she described herself. Hard working. Obedient. Reliable. Eager to do whatever the elders asked her to do, whether it was to run to the store to get fresh mangos or to clean up stray dog poop.

It took them three months before they formally allowed her into their dungeon for the first time. She was the proverbial kinky kid in the kinky candy store, running around and squealing at their voluminous array of equipment. This charmed them, and they teased her about the terrible things that could happen to a sub in there.

"I know," she said coyly. "I mean, wow, this paddle!" She held up a unique double-sided toy made of metal and wood. "That would really hurt!"

"I made it myself," Leon said proudly. "That's why you've never seen one like it."

"The studded side is wild," Marla said. "It must hurt like crazy."

"Would you like to find out?" Milli asked. "Because my inner service top would like to show you how it feels."

They all laughed except Marla, who got into a kneeling position and clasped her hands. "Yes, Ms. Milli, would you please show me?"

After that, they did what kinky people do together. They spent the whole night showing her their toys and using them on her. Marla was in a trance of delight, soaking up each sensation with sighs and moans, writhing like tall grasses in high winds. The elders quietly admired her appetite and her endurance. She was the real thing, alright.

When she was finally tired out, they held her hands and caressed her cheeks, stroking her like a little lamb, while she repeated, "Thank you," so many times and with such tearful gratitude that they melted. It was official: she was part of their family. They were fully attached now.

That night, Gigi gave her a delicate black chain with a small lock on it.

"This is a training collar, a collar of protection, nothing more." She attached it around Marla's neck. "In three more months, if we all agree, we'll see about making it more permanent. But no promises or expectations, let's just see if we all work together."

"I understand, Mistress Gigi. Thank you, Mistress. Thank you, thank you. I felt invisible, but now I feel seen." The elders circled her and raised her to her feet for a group hug.

At the end of her probation, Marla asked for a permanent collar and they granted it. And then Marla shocked them with a request they never saw coming.

"Please may I introduce you to Berry? I know you'll like them," Marla told Gigi. "They'll fit right in!"

"What kind of berry? Blue? Straw?"

"Berry is a kinky friend of mine who lives in Denver."

"A romantic interest?" Gigi asked.

"Oh no, another submissive! I'll vouch for them."

"Is Berry one person or two?"

"Berry is non-binary and their pronouns are they or them."

"I see," said Gigi, but she didn't.

Milli Googled it for them after Marla left. "Them is the pronoun to refer to people who are non-binary, so you don't address them as a single gender."

"Well, what's non-binary? Both genders or neither?"

"Both," Milli kept reading, "but wait, it could also mean neither."

"Wow, I feel really old now," Leon said. "I never even heard of that."

"Right?" Milli said. "It's like a whole new world now! A better world, if you ask me."

Leon was reading over her shoulder. "Holy shit, I should've been a them all along!"

"Your gender is slut," Gigi said. "Anyway, enough Internet for tonight."

Marla brought Berry for a visit the next weekend.

"My pronouns are they/them," Berry announced when introduced. Berry was a slender androgynous 30-year-old with baby blue eyes, a scarred upper lip, and mismatched clothes. They moved gracefully like a ballet dancer and had a beautiful smile. Their teeth were so white they seemed to light the room when Berry grinned. "I am 100% a service sub. Also, asexual."

"Which means what, exactly?" Milli asked.

"I don't do sex with people."

"Jesus Christ, kid, at our age, we don't do sex with them either," Gigi said.

"Ok, cool, cool," Berry said. "So am I in?"

Marla spoke up. "Berry, I told you there has to be probation first, nobody is going to let you into their family without a long trial period." She looked at Gigi. "Isn't that right, Ma'am?"

"Absolutely right."

Berry blushed. They knew the rules but had hoped to get a pass on the probation part.

The new kid made Gigi almost giddy. It was like the old days when she had subs and slaves coming and going all the time, but what the actual fuck was going on here? This influx of young people shocked her to the core -- and yet it touched her in a place that hadn't been touched in 40 years. They were smart and earnest and cute, naïve, so sweet in their sincere hunger to serve. Almost pure, really. People like them had always been hard to find.

Berry lived about 50 miles from them, in an apartment they shared with two roommates. Berry was an architect who did consulting work from home, but the roommates were "normies" -- another new term to the elders, who called them "vanillas." The roomies turned mean and distant when Berry began to embrace a non-binary identity. At first, they used to invite Berry to their bar nights and parties, but the more colorful Berry's outfits became, the fewer invitations the roomies extended. Berry wasn't angry, just lonely and bored.

Berry followed Marla's lead by being as useful as possible, doing everything they could think of to make life easier for the elders. Berry brought something special to the mix: expert carpentry skills and a sharp eye for aesthetic and practical improvements. Sleek rails and sturdy ramps began popping up, making the house safer and more livable for aging adults.

Berry was like a clairvoyant of future house disasters.

"Look at that step," Berry would say, inspecting the main stairs top to bottom. "One day, someone will trip on that step," they said, "and some of the balusters are loose."

"Did you say the ballbusters are loose?" Leon asked.

"BA-LOO-STERS," Berry replied in innocence.

With two youngsters hooking their chains to the elders' carts, it only made sense when Marla and Berry suggested a third possible addition to the household.

"Magenta is a genius," Marla said. "We found her on Twitch! You have to meet her, really. Berry and I have become best friends with her."

"Is Twitch a porn site?" Milli turned to Leon. "Do you think people have fetishes for twitches?"

"What? No!" Marla said. "Twitch is just for fun. Berry and I met Magenta in the Dungeons and Dragons community."

"Come on," Milli said, "even that sounds kinky."

Berry said, "It kind of is but it really isn't."

"That fully answers the question," Gigi said, and they moved on to talk about Magenta.

A week later, Magenta sat down to be vetted in the kitchen. She was in her early fifties and very polite.

"My pronouns are her and she," she announced. "I prefer you call me Magenta, but I won't get pissed off if you accidentally deadname me or use the wrong pronoun."

"Remind me what a deadname is." Gigi heard that word before but wasn't sure what it meant.

"A deadname is the name you had in a different life, when you were a different person, and now that you've moved on, you don't even identify with the old name because you aren't that person anymore."

Leon raised his eyebrows at Gigi. She knew what he was thinking: that Lucinda was Gigi's deadname and she hated when people still used Lucinda. She barely identified with the old version of herself. Gigi felt that she was a better, saner version of that other person who had made so many mistakes and broken so many hearts.

"Kink-aligned?" Milli guessed.

"Heavy bottom, pain slut, masochist," Magenta said. "Needle play, scarification, trampling, electro-play. I know you'll put me on probation. That's cool."

Like Marla, Magenta had relocated during COVID but for work reasons, not personal ones. She came to Colorado to teach botany at a local college. She was really too good for the school, but as a transwoman it was impossible for her to find a teaching job at a big college, so she settled for one at a small, private one in Boulder.

She arrived in Colorado when everything was closing up, including the bars and clubs. So she took all her interests online, where she met Marla and Berry.

She lived in the basement of a middle-class home owned by a family who let her sign the lease sight unseen. They didn't ask about her gender identity so she didn't say anything about it. That was a mistake. When she showed up, they didn't want to give her the key. But she had the contract and the law on her side and called the cops when the landlord wouldn't let her in. The cops reluctantly explained that they would have to take Magenta to court to get out of their contract or face jail time. At that they relented but, as she put it, a malevolent aura hung over them. They spied on her, they tried to keep her a secret from the neighbors, and when their kids said hello to her, they got punished. Magenta planned to get out as soon as the lease was up. Of all the youngers, Magenta was by far the most worldly and the most grounded in reality. She was weary with disappointment, but still friendly and kind.

At first, they kept it casual with Magenta. Since she was in her 50s, they decided to treat her more like a play buddy and did not offer her a collar. It turned out Magenta was a fantastic player, the kind of masochist that sadistic dreams were made of.

She had only one boundary: no full nudity, nothing below the waist in front. Otherwise, she was the ultimate pain-slut and body adventurer.

She started showing up every weekend and slept on an air mattress in their empty finished basement. She volunteered to do whatever chores Gigi thought up but mostly helped Marla and Berry with their chores. She also spent a lot of time poking around their overgrown backyard.

One day Magenta said, "May I have the privilege of turning your backyard into the garden you deserve? I only get to play with plants and soil at school. I miss working in my old garden back home. Do you trust me enough to believe I'll give you a beautiful space?"

"You think you could tame that jungle out there?" Leon asked.

"Oh, definitely," Magenta said. "All it takes is back-breaking work and endless frustration. I'm up for it!"

"God, I can't believe how masochistic you are!" Marla said. "I'm jealous!"

"You're a dream come true," Gigi told Magenta. "We thought the patio was enough, but now that there are six of us and a whole pack of dogs every weekend, it would be nice to have more space to spread out in the back."

"Say no more," Magenta chirped. "I'm on it. If I may, I'd like to improve your greenhouse too. Not to step on any toes, but your pot plants could be doing better. I'd like to work on them first so we get them producing better buds."

"Absolutely." The elders were pleased to support her botanical skills. "Go right ahead."

Magenta's plans for the abandoned gardens and orchards captivated them. "I'll put benches here, in the gulch, and turn it into a rose garden. Berry, we should put some ramps in on both sides for easy in and out."

"Ramps, check," Berry said.

It all happened so fast. One day they were a threesome and now they were a sixsome.

Soon, Magenta and Berry showed up every Friday and didn't leave until Sunday evening. Berry begged to stay in the attic, which had bare wood walls and a big window overlooking the neighborhood. Magenta replaced the couch with a daybed in the basement and added a couple of tables and plants to make it look homier. Marla saw them all week long and would go back to her place to sleep. The Corgis came with her, and their old dogs took a liking to the old Corgis. Suddenly, four formerly elderly dogs were playing like puppies together.

And so the entire house came to life, as if it had been waiting its whole life for a big, happy family to inhabit it.

"The kids really know what they're doing," Leon observed as they sat in lawn chairs one warm Sunday afternoon, watching the youngers digging deep holes for the rosebushes.

"You do know that Magenta is older than Jax, right?" Milli said. "She isn't a kid."

"But they're our kids, so they'll always be kids to us."

"What kind of circular reasoning is that?"

"I'm a round peg in a square hole," Leon replied.

"They're not our kids, they are our free labor," Milli said, toking on a pipe. "Holy shit, the new pot is really great!"

"Free, my ass," Gigi said. "Have you seen our food bills lately?"

"You don't have to spoil them with gourmet stuff, do you?" Leon teased.

"They call it ethical food. Who knew having ethics could be so expensive? Listen, they're not our kids or our free laborers. They are our younger companions," Gigi said. "We provide a safe space in exchange for their service, but we are a stopping station on their journeys, not their final destination."

Once she said those words, the elders all got melancholy. Gigi wished she could take the words back but they were true. The six of them found a peaceful and productive way to live across generations but it would not last. It couldn't. Mortality was knocking at their door.

"It sucks we only get to see them all on weekends," Milli said.

"We could let Magenta move into the basement full-time," Leon said. "Berry could turn it into a little paradise for her."

"And what about Berry? We can't let them stay with the asshat roomies."

"Berry has the attic!" Leon said. "They could even pay some nominal rent. Then we could buy them more ethical food."

"Anything else?" Gigi couldn't believe her little clan was ready for this. Was she? She wasn't sure.

"We can leave them the house when we're gone," Milli said. "We don't have any other heirs."

"You know, that's the best idea you've ever had," said Leon.

"Wow!" Gigi muttered. "Just wow."

The whole thing sounded crazy. But it also made sense. Why not let them move in? My God. Was she losing her mind?

There was room for Marla too, if she was tired of the shed. Her aunt probably wouldn't even know she was gone. In fact, the aunt wouldn't know if the Corgis were gone, either. Marla had reported that her aunt had dramatically declined over the last eight months. She didn't recognize Marla or even her nurse. Marla wasn't sure what would happen if the aunt died, but she was pretty sure the aunt would leave the house to her church, and Marla would either have to find an apartment here or take the dogs to Michigan. Either way, she'd need a full-time job. She saw the logic in making their younger friends the heirs to the house, but it was all happening too fast for her. What if they were wrong about the kids? What if the kids knew they were in the will and got greedy and evil?

She called Jax as soon as she got into bed that night, and launched into a monologue about how moving them in and then giving them legal rights to the property after their death was crazy, risky, maybe stupid. They could end up broke or abused if one of the youngers got greedy and wanted them gone. What if the neighbors caught on? All six of them could get run out of the neighborhood. They'd be more visible and thus more vulnerable.

"It's a terrible idea with terrifying possibilities," Gigi said.

"Aww, it sounds like a great idea with wonderful potential for all! A solid safe space for the youngers and a safer, jollier space for the elders!"

"You mean it?"

"I do! It's an elegant solution for everyone. I don't think it's moving too fast. Marla's already been with you almost a year, right? Berry and Magenta are amazing. It's a beautiful thing. What's better than kinky partners who love you? Extra Bonus: they'll be there to help you when you get infirm."

"That's my fear," Gigi said. "They'll get stuck taking care of us. That doesn't seem fair at all to them."

"It isn't stuck when you do it by choice," Jax said. "Then it's an act of love."

Gigi's tired old heart lifted. Jax might as well have been talking about herself. Her loyalty had gotten Gigi's triad through many dark times. They could never have gotten this house or found this amazing new life in Colorado without her.

Anything was possible where there was dedication and caring. She focused on positive thoughts. Wasn't she lucky to have found young people who wanted to belong to a kinky family? Wasn't she blessed to have a home full of fun and mutual support? Wouldn't it be endearing to live together, share meals together, celebrate holidays together? Of course, it would! Each of them got a little emotional on Sundays when it was time to part. So why did they need to part? They were good to each other. They were good for each other. She had seen their hearts through their actions. They didn't have a mean bone in them. She knew they would never hurt Leon or Milli, and least of all her, who they treated like a Mother Goddess.

Gigi embraced Jax's wisdom. It was up to Gigi to stop thinking like a broken old woman, to forget past miseries and heartbreaks, and time to look forward to savoring the gifts destiny had miraculously bestowed.

The future was not dark and coldly predictable. The future was gaping wide with glorious new possibilities.

☙ Chapter 9 ❧

A VISION OF LOVE

Sometimes we have to lose ourselves to truly find ourselves. We have to move in new ways and listen to new songs, to reach for distant stars but keep our feet planted on Mother Earth. We have to reject what we hate about ourselves and embrace our best qualities. For Corey, finding himself meant resolving his inner war with art. He needed a stronger foundation to break out of the prison of the past and step into his destiny. To become who he wanted to be required self-love and self-mastery above all.

Corey squatted in front of a 4-foot wide, 3-foot thick, 6-foot tall smoothly sanded block of basswood. He's been staring at it for three hours, periodically moving his chair around to study its contours from different perspectives. Indifferent motherfucker. It was blank. It was nothing inside of nothingness, a mirror of his deficient imagination.

It felt so yielding in his hands at first. The sawdust flew softly as if shedding skin to reveal the soul within. For weeks, he sanded in a state of euphoria. But the moment he started to chisel, the wood closed up like a tomb.

Jax would be shocked at how much cash he blew on the wood. Transporting it to the apartment cost almost as much. At the time, he got it deep in his head that this gorgeous indulgence would bring an end to his creative block. Now he wanted to chop it all up into firewood. He stared with helpless rage.

"You worthless piece of shit." He pounded the vast vertical column and kicked over the stepladder beside it. "You fucking ugly motherfucker."

He sat down awkwardly and crossed his arms. He was the asshole, blaming the wood. That's what Reddit would say: YTA (you're the asshole). It wasn't the materials. It was the artist. It was always the artist.

Objectively, the wood was uncommonly large and beautiful. From its death, he had hungered to salvage its beauty and make it even more beautiful. But he lacked the vision to bring forth its secrets. He felt guilty that a living tree gave its life to human greed only to end up abandoned in an art studio.

But what form? It didn't want to be what he wanted to be, a regal, six-foot-tall statue of his wife. A tribute to her womanly power. To make her as powerful in clothes as Moore's statue was in its nakedness.

He carried his coffee back to the kitchen. The kids had more creativity than he did. Miranda's posters were bold and experimental. Zane showed a real talent for Anime. How easily it came to them. Sit them down with paper and crayons and they could produce one picture after another, proud of each. They believed in their work.

He missed them. Their footsteps hammering the floors, their messes, their squeals and shouts echoing through the house, their freshly washed faces at the dinner table, their little arms around his neck. Jax and the kids were gone for a few days, visiting with Gigi and her clan in Colorado. Even the dogs had abandoned him. Jax brought them to their favorite Pet Spa and Resort while she was away.

Corey saw them all off with smiles and hugs, calm and collected, so they wouldn't know he felt spooky-sad on the inside. The house was a crypt without them. He missed his kids and he missed his woman. Without them, his reason for living was gone.

Corey never would have guessed it while he was single, but creating in the midst of a bustling home revolutionized his process. He was born for the dirt and mess of life, the chaos, the sudden interruptions, and the last-minute changes in plans. He could never be the isolated, lone wolf working in an atelier. He needed to hear howls of laughter and screams of disappointment in the background, the sounds of footsteps fast and slow, he even needed to smell the meals cooking in the kitchen, and the stink of the dogs when they came into the house on a rainy day.

He popped open his laptop and read the latest headlines. Then he stopped himself from going down all the rabbit holes. He walked back to the bedroom and sat down at his desktop and reached for a cigar in the stash in his lower drawer. He called Marco on Skype.

"Brother!" Marco smiled at him from the screen. He wore a sharp green silk shirt, his hair perfectly styled, his beard immaculately groomed, and his muscles bulging at the sleeve. "What brings you here?"

"Heyee. You are looking very sharp, my friend! So,

spontaneous cigar party, whaddya think?"

"Aw, why the fuck not, sure." Marco sprang to his feet to search for the right cigar. "That's how to start the day. When you're mentally unstable, I mean."

Marco's boy, Wesley, came running through the room in the background. He was wearing what looked like half a chicken. Corey squinted at the bright yellow panties with big ruffles all over.

"What the fuck is Wesley wearing?"

"You mean the horror panties?"

"Are you trying to decondition him from crossdressing? Because, I gotta say, those are butt ugly."

"Literally!" Marco was gleeful. "He's being punished. Boy did a bad, bad thing yesterday. He blew up my credit card at Target."

"Oh, no, what did he buy?"

"Enough plushies to fill his room. Don't even get me started. His excuses were hilarious, though. He was trying to push my buttons."

"See, this is what I like about Pro-Domming. Don't have to put up with submissive shit."

"Like the shit you give Jax?"

Corey winced. "Uh-huh, exactly like that." He paused. "How's the health?"

"Doctor's happy, and so am I. The negative viral load is durable. She said if I keep doing what I'm doing, I could outlive her." He laughed. "And she's only 30!"

Corey sighed in relief. "Do it! Outlive her! Outlive all of us."

"Well, that's a disconcerting concept but thank you." Marco leaned back in his chair. "I spent yesterday looking at properties with Jax, and the kids came along for the ride. They are growing up too fast, those two. I couldn't believe how much Zane has grown since I saw them a few months ago. He'll be taller than you one day. And do I see traces of a fuzzy mustache coming in?"

"Oh, yeah," Corey grinned. "He is deep into puberty -- and Jax is deep in stiff socks." They gaped at each other in amusement. "So did you tell my esteemed wife whether you want to keep doing Pro-Dom or what?"

"I told her I want to move to real estate full-time. It's almost full-time already, so might as well make it official and work out a new business plan. Economically, it makes sense for us now."

"Oh, I'll miss sharing the space with you, brother. But I support you totally. How did Jax take it, though?"

"She agreed with me that it was a good move. She said Denver could be the solution to a lot of different problems, in fact."

"Nice! Glad it went so well, Marco, congrats! I know it's what you wanted, buddy."

"You know I always wanted to be a real estate mogul."

"I do, I do."

"Well, there's a bit more to it. I don't know if she told you..."

"I'm sure she'll fill me in," Corey shrugged.

"Yeah. OK, well, one way or another, I would've quit. Once I found my Wesley and Lloyd, I kind of lost interest in doing strangers. I didn't realize it at first, but the kind of emotional reward I get out of being with people I know love me, I can't get that with strangers."

"Yeah, I get it. It definitely hits differently with someone you love."

"Very much so," Marco said. "Plus, you know, it's not like you get to pick your strangers, you just deal with whatever comes through the door and every now and then, it's kind of demoralizing when you know you would never touch them in real life."

"I feel that," Corey nodded. "Can't do a great scene with a bad player."

"Right? Or a smelly one. Ugh."

"Oh yeah, that's the worst. Hygiene matters!"

"Exactly. It's not like our private parties, where we pick who we let in. That's still fun. But, yeah, no more Pro-Domming for me unless I feel broke again."

"I hear you. I don't know how long it'll last for me, but I'm still into it. I didn't get a lot of submissive play before I met Jax, and I definitely didn't get my topping game together either. So this has been an education. It's like the more I learn about people, the more I learn about myself."

"Like what? What's something you learned about yourself?"

Corey paused. "Well, I used to be brattier with Jax. I kind of wanted her to tame me into it, even when I was the one asking for it."

"Why do you think that is?"

"Shame, maybe? Like as a man, I have to pretend to put up a fight."

"Or Mommy issues?" Marco said. "I mean. Your mom. Whoooo."

"Yeah, maybe," Corey said. He didn't want to blame all his problems on his mother, but, fuck, she was the root of a lot of them. He knew it. His wife knew it. And so did Marco.

"Anyway, it amazes me how my clients can just surrender

like BOOM. They dive into subspace like it was a heated pool. That surprised me, so I asked myself, 'Why are they able to instantly surrender to a stranger when it's so hard for me to go into subspace with Jax?'"

"You've put on some great shows for us, though."

"Yeah, but when we're alone, it's different. In public, it gets a little performative because I don't want to disrespect her, you know, but on the inside, I feel like it's weak to just surrender. I should have some fight in me."

"The captive stallion? Unwilling victim?"

"Something like that. I know it's fucked up."

"Cut yourself some slack, buddy. It's not uncommon to want to be forced into something -- even when you're the one who asked for it in the first place." Marco laughed softly.

"Right? I ask for something, and then when she starts doing it, I act like I need to be forced into it. Like, what if I just surrendered?"

"What a concept! Surrendering to your Dominant! What will you subs think of next?"

"You can't imagine."

"Oh, yes, I think I can!"

"Anyway, I'm working on it, trying to let myself be more vulnerable." Corey stubbed out his cigar. "She's noticed it and it seems to make it even hotter for her."

"Interesting... a Dom turned on by an eager sub. Who woulda thunk it?" Then he peered at Corey's short cigar. "What is that? A Groundhog?"

"Yep. Short, but powerful. What are you smoking?"

"A Don Carlos Eye of the Shark." Marco waved it proudly.

"Wow, I guess real estate really is profitable."

"Darling, you would not believe how profitable! I'm part of the gay real estate network here now and we get the hottest leads thanks to a bunch of gossip queens. Plus, you know, we're all pulling for each other. You know the price Gigi got. She couldn't have touched that property three years ago. Now there are fire sales every week. Unvaccinated Boomers are dropping like flies around here."

"Ok, wait. We're profiting off MAGA deaths? That's kind of... macabre. Albeit, a little grimly satisfying."

"The irony is that homos are snapping up properties once owned by homophobes. A strange kind of Divine Providence is at work in the Heartland."

"Oh, no, no, no, no," Corey choked with laughter.

"But honestly, it's really the heirs who get the big profit. We only get a small fraction." Marco puffed calmly. "And, let me tell you, those heirs are destroying home values in some neighborhoods by competitive price-slashing so they can grab the cash and go."

"Wow, that's really sad."

"It's bad for business, if you ask me. God only knows where the economy will land after COVID is over. IF it's ever over. But you're in the pink, my friend. Me and Jax are going to make some big bucks off their poor choices. So take heart, you'll have plenty to spend on art materials."

"Fuck art materials." The minute he said it, he regretted saying those words out loud. He'd whined enough to Marco about his creative slump. He looked away and re-lit his cigar.

"Ohhhhh. I see. So you didn't call me to moan about your family being here instead of there. You called because you can't get your arty ass in gear."

"The gear fell off, I think. I don't know if it'll ever come back."

They puffed in moody silence.

"It will," Marco suddenly pronounced.

"What? Just like that, huh?"

"I have a premonition." His friend fanned out his hands as if parting heavy curtains and said, "I see Corey working at what he loves without the baggage of shame and inadequacy, without imposter's syndrome. The sculptor will sculpt again. I can see it now." Marco closed his eyes. "Yes, I see the massive shoulders of an artist straining to summon beauty forth. I see powerful biceps and triceps rippling, and a fine, round ass flexing its muscles, bubblicious butt cheeks beckoning..."

"Oh shut up." Corey couldn't hold back his laughter. "Come on, man."

"Ha! I thought you were bisexual now?"

"Hetero-flexible! Or is that bi-flexible? I forget. But, listen, if I have to blow you to convince you."

"I'll keep that in mind," Marco said, sucking in his cheeks. "Not sure your lovely wife would go for that, but..."

"Are you kidding? She'd set it up."

"Oh my God," Marco said, "you're probably right about that."

Wesley appeared once more. Now he was in jeans and a T-shirt. "Master?"

"Aw, shit, honey," Marco apologized to Corey, "I've got to get going. We're supposed to look at a friend's house to see whether he is ready to sell. Jax was over the moon when she saw it, so we'll see if he's ready to let it go. He'll have to sell below his original asking because the market's crashed near him, but I'm working my magic on him."

"Oh, yeah?" Corey tried to sound interested, but real estate was his wife's fetish. The only part he cared about was whether it made her and Marco happy.

"It's a gorgeous space," Marco said.

"Uh-huh, sounds very nice."

Wesley brought in the big guns now. He dragged Lloyd over. Lloyd was a woolly mammoth of a bear in his 60s, with a crew cut and long white beard. Lloyd was once Marco's Daddy, then his fuck-buddy, and now his slave. He was a twinkly-eyed guy with a big, handsome nose and a bald, handsome head. A big hairy slave with big shaved balls.

"Sir, it's time to go. Now," he said with quiet authority.

"My slaves have ganged up on me!"

"I see that."

"Ta-ta, big guy, I'll catch you later."

Corey closed the Skype room and sat back in his chair, draping his long legs over the armrests. Kink relationships were fucking hilarious. So juicy! So filled with the raw materials of life.

* * *

How Lloyd and Marco's relationship had evolved over the last 20 years always gave him food for thought. Going from top to bottom or bottom to top, he'd seen that plenty of times. But getting to watch a Master/slave dynamic evolve so profoundly was fantastic. Daddy Lloyd and then-boy Marco first popped onto his radar at a Leather Pride parade in Boston the year before Corey met Jax.

Corey had quit his lawyer job, and his mother had been verbally beating him up about it, calling him at odd hours to shriek about her disappointment and how embarrassed she was to tell her friends about her loser son. He escaped to his father David's place in Provincetown and apprenticed in his art studio. Living with David taught him all kinds of unexpected things about gay culture. Gay men were so much freer in spirit, so much freer with affection than straight people, and totally out about kink and Leather. To the repressed Catholic boy Corey once was, gay culture spoke directly to his secret wishes and dreams for a more sexually liberated world. When David made his annual pilgrimage to Boston Pride, Corey tagged along. Dad had made it clear he would be seeing old friends and going to clubs, so they agreed they'd meet back at the hotel at some point that night and head home the next day.

Corey wandered through the familiar streets of Boston and then merged into the unfamiliar crowds of gays and lesbians waiting eagerly to watch the parade. He took photos with his mind of the sheer exuberant energy all around him.

He spotted his Doppelganger -- a man around his height, dressed in an identical white tank, tight black jeans, the same model of Wesco boots, and the same crew cut. The only difference was that his look-alike wore a thick steel chain around his neck with a Masterlock on it. Corey eyed the mark of ownership with envy. He couldn't imagine walking around in public with a visible chain. His Doppelganger noticed him too and walked up to him.

"Hello, brother," he said, "what's your name?"

"Corey," he told him, "and yours?"

"Marco. I'm here with my Master." Marco pointed to an older man smoking a cigar and talking to some other older men. "Are you here with anyone?"

"Well, I drove down from Provincetown with my dad."

"Awwww! Is he here to support you? How cute, I love it."

"Actually, I'm the supporter," Corey said. "Dad's the gay guy in the family." He laughed.

"No shit. So why are you dressed like me?" Marco teased him.

"Well, I'm sub." Corey couldn't believe he'd said something so dumb. Also, he couldn't believe he said it out loud. It thrilled him that Marco didn't even blink.

"Ah! You're a hetero leather guy? Nice. So you really are my brother!"

Corey instantly felt at ease. Marco was so nice, so open. "I guess I am!"

"Come here, honey," Marco said, giving him a hug. Corey didn't know what to feel but he was grateful for the hug. The two climbed a grassy hill nearby and smoked a blunt together. They told each other their whole life stories in short, rapid-fire sentences. Marco was raised on a cattle ranch in Colorado. His parents kicked him out for being gay. He moved to Boston broke and terrified, then God led him to the Eagle where he met Master Lloyd. He was into softball, martial arts, and kayaking. He wanted to own land one day. Lots of land. Master Lloyd was supporting him while he studied to get his real estate license.

Aside from looking alike, they did not have a whole lot in common, but they liked each other anyway. When they ran out of words, Corey nudged his shoulder. Marco pushed back. Then they started rolling around on the grass and suddenly rolled all the way down the hill, laughing and screaming as they clung to each other. When they finally came to a stop, Daddy Lloyd was waiting for them. They were stained green from head to toe, like a couple of kids who got into some paint.

"I see you turned into elves while I was gone," Lloyd said, a faint smile twitching on his lips.

"That's us!" Corey was too exhilarated to contain himself. "The Two Kinky Elves!"

"Kinky Elves!" Marco echoed. "That should be the name of a band!"

Lloyd rolled his eyes at them, and they had a good laugh. They were best friends from then on.

It was a wonderful way for Corey to connect with the bigger world of BDSM. He didn't know what his path would be, he just knew that one day he wanted to feel as free as Marco.

* * *

Corey checked the time and shut his computer. It was dinner time.

He patiently chopped a mountain of tomatoes, onions, zucchini, and jalapenos, then simmered it, stirring idly and finally pouring it on top of a fresh pot of brown rice. He grabbed a big wooden spoon Jax once used for a spanking scene, then sat down to eat it, a couple of bottles of beer at hand. When he finished those, he got a bottle of Shiraz from a cupboard and sliced a chunk of Gouda to go with it.

Now he didn't feel like much. Not good, not bad, just there. He fished the remnants of his cigar from his back pocket. It looked like a flat turd in his palm. It still tasted good, though. He was bloated, replete, tired and glued to the chair. He felt like sleeping in his chair, anything to avoid the empty bed waiting for him. But he had to take a piss or he'd explode, so he labored to his feet and walked to the bathroom next door to his studio.

As he passed, the huge hunk of basswood flashed in the corner of his eye. He thought about Marco's premonition. He knew Marco only said it to make him feel better, to give him a boost to get back to work. But... Maybe Marco sensed he was ready to get back to it. Marco's instincts about him were freakishly keen -- he often sensed when Corey was entering a slump before Corey did. Maybe now he could tell that Corey was ready to break out of one.

He did give up too quickly this morning in the studio. His childhood problems were crippling him. Broken family, a mean stepfather, a Karen for a mother, suffocating Catholic schools, and a sweet but distant gay dad who his mother contemptuously called "the flaming fairy."

What did Marco call it -- imposter's syndrome! Oh yeah. He had a lot of that. As long as he could remember he was always pretending to be things he was not. Imposter obedient son. Imposter choir boy. Imposter lawyer. He never felt free to say the things he thought and felt, he was never allowed to be anything but a good boy. Now he felt like an imposter artist.

It diminished some when he met Jax. She allowed him to be his real self and he definitely felt like a real husband and father at home. But when it came to work, he just tried to go along to get along. At first, becoming an artist seemed like his true vocation, but he carried the fear that he was just doing art to please his father, even after the old man was in the grave. Fuck, he hated himself. That was the problem. He loved his wife and kids, he loved his friends, and he hated himself.

He finished up in the bathroom and walked warily into his studio. He should've been thinking about the statue, but all he could think about was Jax.

* * *

He remembered their first summer together in Provincetown. When he glimpsed her on the beach from a distance she looked like a movie actress. He expected cameras and a director to suddenly swoop in. Then his father recognized the old dude with Jax and said they should go say hi because that was the man whose welcoming party they were going to down the road.

"Paul! Paul!" his dad cried, and the two old guys ran to each other and embraced like old lovers. It wasn't the first time his dad bumped into an old boyfriend, but it was definitely the first time he made out with one in front of his son.

Corey turned his attention to the beautiful woman. The closer he got, the more beautiful she was. A goddess incarnate, from her clear ivory skin and penetrating gray eyes to her shapely breasts, full hips, and long curvy legs. Her hair was a wild mass of blond curls. Her locks flowed symmetrically as if carved. She wore a simple pale blue shirt and worn blue jeans. Lustrous grey pearls dangled from her earlobes on delicate silver chains. She moved like the ocean waves, her body was fluid and relaxed, each pose photographable. She pulled some locks of hair off her face and caught him staring. She smiled, then her lips curled into a smirk. He had an out-of-body experience. He felt a mad urge to drop to his knees and kiss her feet right then.

He never had the kind of balls he summoned up that day, never before or since. He never wanted a woman as much as he wanted her either. She told him she was kinky and he told her he was too and, by some miracle, she agreed to go on a date with him. It was terrifying and exhilarating at the same time. He never believed he'd find a woman he wanted to marry. He never believed he'd find the RIGHT woman to marry. She was HER. He felt it in his guts.

They went on a first date, then a second and a third. They fell into a rhythm, and it was almost too good to be real. A month later, the rhythm broke, and things got bad. Really bad.

Then it came back and everything was right again, but not as right as before. He didn't know why, exactly, but she was mad at him all the time. Just like his mother. He didn't text her as much. Soon, she wasn't texting him back at all. He got frantic and started texting her constantly.

She responded but it wasn't the response he'd hoped for.

"Don't love-bomb me," she wrote. "It never leads to anything good."

He didn't think he was love-bombing her. He was trying to show her he really cared. Maybe he seemed a little needy, but don't subs get to be needy? He was insulted. She misunderstood him. She was like all the rest, another bitch inside an angel's body. He sulked and told himself he was done with her bullshit. He couldn't handle it anymore.

But a few days later, he went back to texting her. This time, she didn't text back for a week, so he tried calling her. When she blocked his phone calls, he fell into a depression. He thought he'd lost her forever. What had he done?? He excoriated himself. What kind of asshole bombards their girlfriend, much less their Dominant girlfriend? She was right. He was the problem. He got scared of how fast it was going and pulled away. Then he got scared of losing her and pushed her too hard.

He wrote her a long letter in a shaky hand and delivered it to the place where she and Paul were staying for the summer. He told her he never meant to control her. That was the last thing he wanted. He wanted to be a better man for her. If she would only give him another chance, he would prove his love to her every day for the rest of their lives. She was everything he'd ever hoped to find in a woman and more. He wanted to be her slave. He would do anything to earn back her trust.

An agonizing three days later, she texted him back. She told him to meet her for dinner at their favorite crab shack. He got there early so he could wait for her in the parking lot. As soon as she stepped out of the funky old cab she had driven from New York to the Cape, he ran to her and dropped to his knees. Right there in the parking lot. He didn't care who saw him. He half-expected God to strike him dead. Instead, he won her forgiveness, and Jax said she missed him too. She was sorry for being so hard on him. She had her own relationship baggage to deal with, she said. She forgave him. They should try again. There was something real between them. He didn't cry but he wanted to.

That night, she put him on a three-month probation. Six weeks later, the probation ended by her decree. They had found a powerful permanently smooth rhythm together. It felt right, and it stayed right for them. Their near break-up was their first and last significant fight. Now they'd been married for almost thirteen years, with two great kids, and they were closer than ever. He did not fail her; he became a better man for her.

* * *

If he could be a better man for Jax, why, why, couldn't he be a better artist for himself? Why couldn't he do for himself what he always tried to do for her -- to step up to the plate, push himself to new levels of excellence, and forge on with confidence?

Corey swigged a big sip of wine and went back to brooding about the basswood. His thoughts were starting to organize a little. He had the skills. He had the energy. Now he needed the vision. You cannot undertake a sculpture without having a vision of where you want it to go. He'd wasted whole blocks of wood trying to impose forms they weren't made for. Clearly, the wood didn't want to be a tall statue of his wife. It wanted something else. Maybe it wanted to be on its side, less like a tower and more like a landscape.

He carefully lowered the wood into a horizontal position on the wide plinth. Now it looked like a huge fish. He was trying to imagine Jax crouching like a tiger, hair flying behind her, but it still looked like a fish.

What else looked like a long fish? A torpedo. Or perhaps a boat. The dimensions could work if he carved waves on the bottom and shortened the ends.

He sat back on the chair and let his mind roll back to their boat trip later that first summer, after weeks of blissful play and cozy cuddling in front of campfires on the beach.

* * *

Temperatures were already cooling off. Soon, it would be Fall. Jax was still trying to decide whether to return to New York to take care of their apartment and their cats, or if she'd stay with Paul in Provincetown through the winter. Paul had finally decided to accept David's offer that they move into his place for the winter. Corey didn't want to pressure Jax, but if she went home to New York, their rhythm could die. It would be the worst winter of his life if she left.

He proposed they escape for a few days, just the two of them. He would borrow a sailboat from a local guy who owed him some legal work. It had sleeping quarters downstairs and a basic kitchen. It wasn't a yacht, but it was classy. They could sail to a quiet bay, maybe around Falmouth, and set anchor far from the escalating curiosity of Paul and David's friends, who kept asking when "the kids" were getting married and whether they were planning to have children. The pressure of it, when he still didn't know if she'd stay or go, was killing him.

The boat trip was perfect, permanently etched into his memory down to its slightest detail. Until they had Zane and then Miranda, he'd never known such happiness. Nights of moonlight, wine, and deep conversations that led to confessions and revelations that led to sex and bondage. They'd hasten to the cabin below where she tormented him for hours of mad ecstasy. It was easier to surrender to her then, too, he realized with a jolt. Was it the newness of their passion that had freed him? Or the realization that he had found The One.

On their last night out there was a full moon. It cast an argentine glow on the deck.

Jax said, "Let's play in this gorgeous silver light! No one will be able to see us."

He agreed with some apprehension. What if a patrol boat came by? What if another sailboat showed up? But he followed her lead obediently, carrying the ropes she ordered him to bring.

"I want to tie you to the mast, like in the pirate movies I watched as a kid."

"I don't know," he said, though his heart was racing with anticipation. "I'm not sure it's a good idea."

"It's a wonderful idea," she said. She tied him to the mast, leaving his pants on lest an unexpected visitor show up.

"How will you explain the bondage?"

"Why would I have to? We're adults." Then she paused. "I can tell them I'm learning sailing knots and experimenting on you."

"Like they'd believe that."

"People believe what they want to believe, regardless of

what they see. So that's on them. I'll give them a plausible explanation, but I'm not responsible for their imagination."

"Yes, Ma'am," he said. "I'll tell them you forced me to be your guinea pig."

"Am I forcing you?"

"A little. But in all good ways."

"Good. Then shut up."

With his back bare and vulnerable, the winds felt like icy lips on his skin. When her whip landed, the ice became fire. He could see nothing but the horizon ahead. He dipped into a trance as the strokes built from mild to near-terrifying. When he finally used his safe word, she dropped the whip and wrapped herself around his back, murmuring softly, "You are so beautiful, so handsome, I love you."

It was the first time she used the L word. He would go to his grave still remembering that moment. He remembered expecting she'd untie him so they could run back down to the cabin. Instead, she untied one wrist and turned him around so he was facing her, then tied his free wrist back to the mast.

Now he could watch her, his beautiful goddess with ferocious hair and dangerous eyes. She wiggled her fingers at him and he gasped. She moved so close that the heat of her large breasts and hard nipples made his insides melt with desire. She played with his nipples and gave him tiny bites in circles from belly to neck. She pressed her groin against his and ground him until his fly was so tight he thought he would spontaneously cum. Then she sprang back laughing because she knew how hard he was. She knew everything about him now. Everything.

"You're not allowed to come yet, slave," she said. "I have more plans for you tonight." He couldn't hold back his orgasm. Her words were like a magic key that unlocked all his inhibitions.

He arched and groaned and wet his jeans with warm, sticky fluid. He was embarrassed, but she seemed tickled.

"You can't help it." She shrugged. "You're a little piggy. You are MY piggy. Do you understand? I own you now."

"Yes, Mistress, yes, yes, I am yours forever."

She untied him. At long last, he gave himself to the urge he'd carried since he first saw her at the beach. He threw himself at her feet. "I love you, Jax, I love you," he said, hugging her calves. "Please marry me, please, I love you so much, please? We were made for each other."

She was stunned. "Wow, Corey, that's... not what I was expecting."

"Wait, I'll be right back. Christ, I almost forgot." He galloped away to the cabin. He rifled nervously through his suitcase, tearing out the clothes still in it, and located the irreplaceable cargo: it was a finely carved black walnut box he'd made for her, with her name on the lid surrounded by shooting stars. Inside the lid, he'd etched: "For the love of my life." He had even bought jeweler's gold and melted it into all the letters. It would be an heirloom they could pass on to their children someday.

He returned to find her leaning over the gunwale, gazing at the sky.

He kneeled behind her and waited for her to turn around.

Jax's face was as mysterious to him now as the Worm Moon that illuminated the deck. A large amethyst set in an 18k gold band sparkled inside the box, like another star in the sky. She lightly ran her finger across the gold-encrusted words.

"This is so beautiful," she murmured. "Museum quality, even."

He shrugged. That wasn't the answer he was hoping for.

"Will you, darling? Will you marry me?"

"Yes, I guess I will," she said, putting the blazing amethyst on her finger and holding her hand up for him to see. "I will marry you."

And oh God, how he swooned then, oh God, yes, how euphoric he felt, never more alive, never happier to be alive. He felt complete. Powerful as a superhero. His back was raw from her whip, his chest aching from her bites, and his mind exploding with rapture. He had everything he wanted, everything he dreamed about since he first laid eyes on Jax.

* * *

That moment changed his life. It was so clear to him now. He needed to transform that moment into art. That's what the wood wanted: it wanted to encapsulate that moment of human ecstasy.

Was it possible to infuse the depth of the emotions he felt that night into this wood? He looked at the wood searchingly. It seemed softer, more yielding, than since he first saw it.

He grabbed a chisel and made the first cut. The wood readily ceded as if it had been waiting to be trimmed in that spot. He made another at the opposite end. It was good. Very good. He caressed it with his palm. It had a kind of sweet mystery to it. He let out an old familiar sigh. That was it. He was in the space. The wood was his ally now. He hugged it for a long moment with gratitude.

He labored with certainty and vigor as if it was what he'd been meant to do all along, to recreate that shining moment when all his worldly questions were resolved by her answer to the only question that really mattered: "Will you marry me?". He let go of his fears and carved freely.

By the time Jax and the kids got back a few days later, he was in full-on creative euphoria, blasting *La donna è mobile* so loud, he didn't hear them enter the house until the kids burst into the studio and cheered. They knew what it meant when Daddy was standing there in dirty clothes, his hands covered in sawdust. Daddy was making art! Jax came up behind them, smiling radiantly. Corey hurriedly threw a tarp on the carving and wiped the sawdust off his hands.

"Daddy, Daddy, Daddy!" the kids yelped. He greeted them effusively, grabbing both of them in his arms and kissing their little cheeks until Zane squirmed away.

"Leave some for me," Jax said merrily.

He unlaced Miranda's arms and straightened up to bear-hug his wife. "I am so happy you are home, darling."

"I am equally happy to be home, darling. Phew, what a week. Too many people, too much sightseeing, I just wanted to be home with you, having our quiet time."

"I want to be in bed with you, but not for quiet time," he declared.

"Shhh!" she said, glancing at the kids.

"Mommy and Daddy love playing Scrabble in bed," he said to them. Jax covered her mouth with her hand. "Speaking of which, who wants Scrabbled Eggs?"

"Yay, yeggs! Bakey, bakey!" Miranda cried for bacon.

He made everyone breakfast for dinner and poured wine for his wife and himself. They toasted each other, their hearts soaring.

That night, after the kids were all tucked in, the weary parents returned to Corey's studio. He couldn't wait to show her the work-in-progress. It had come a long way since she last saw it.

"This studio is suffocating. I hate that you can't even look out a window."

She went to the window facing the air shaft and closed the curtains so they couldn't see the brick wall, only three feet from his sill.

"You deserve a better space."

She was right. The studio wasn't ideal. When he agreed to move back to New York with Jax, he didn't realize how small the apartment would be and how hard it would be to create big pieces in the cramped room. But none of that mattered now.

"Take a look at this, tell me what you think." He pulled the tarp off the statue.

She knew what it was the second she saw it.

"Is that our boat??" she cried. "That's our boat!"

"You see it? You see it already?"

"I see it." She walked up to it to examine it closer. "What beautiful wood. What kind is this?"

"Basswood. Biggest damn chunk of basswood I ever saw. I had to get it." He shrugged apologetically. She nodded. "It was a tad pricey," he added.

"Oh, who cares, you're earning good money now. You deserve a splurge. It is beautiful. You couldn't help but buy it! And you've made such huge, huge progress while I was gone. I am so happy for you, Corey! I'm so proud of you. I think this will be your best work yet!"

"I pulled a few all-nighters," he admitted proudly. "Once I felt the flow..."

"You could not stop." She finished his sentence. "I understand. Paul was like that."

He put his arm around her shoulders, and they watched the statue in silence, as if watching a baby being born.

"That's not us, is it?" she asked, pointing. On the lower right side, he had outlined a man and woman and the base of a mast. The man was prostrate. The woman stood straight, her face tilted up to the moon above. "That's us, isn't it?" she asked again softly.

"Yes. It is us the night I asked you to marry me."

"Oh my God, Corey," she whispered. "Oh, sweetheart."

She touched his face with her fingertips, her gray eyes shining with passion. His cock throbbed uncontrollably. His legs felt weak. They grabbed each other like drowning sailors clinging together on a life raft. In her arms, all of his demons slunk back to their pestilent abysses. The light in her eyes was his North Star.

Life was working out for him after all. All that he experienced, all that he learned, was paying off. Art was in his bones and his wife was in his arms.

❧ Chapter 10 ❧
THE LONG JOURNEY HOME

Apart, we may be strong. But together, we are stronger. Strong enough to overcome hardship and loss, strong enough to weather every storm. Cemented by love and commitment, honor and mutual respect, and kindness above all, they were an indestructible fortress amidst the chaos of life.

J ax stretched her limbs, hands flying over her head and flexed her ankles as far as she could. She arched her back and sunbeams drizzled all over her. The morning was warm and the sun promised a hot day. Her plan was to do fuck all... but with panache.

Early this morning, they all tiptoed out of the house trying not to wake their sleeping guests. She had promised the children that since the weather had finally warmed up, they could have morning swims as long as one of the parents was there to supervise.

Naturally, the kids ran into their bedroom at 6:30 am squealing at their parents, "Are you ready to go? We're ready! Can we go? We can't wait to swim. Swim! Swim!" They were already in their swimsuits.

Corey sprang out of bed, but she pulled the covers over her head and closed her eyes. Corey knew what that meant. He rushed the kids back out of the room and returned a little while later with coffee.

"Ready to face the clan?"

"No." The sun beckoned. The kids were already outside, impatiently waiting for a parent to arrive so they could go in the pool. "But duty calls." She sat up and slid a robe on. "Beautiful day, anyway."

"You don't sound very awake," her husband said. "Are you feeling okay?" He tapped his belly. "Any pain?"

"Not yet."

He shook the pot of coffee. "This will help."

"Just pour the whole pot into my mouth," she said.

"Seriously, you okay?"

"As okay as I was yesterday and the day before that."

"I'm sorry," he said quietly. He sat down on the bed and caressed her forehead. "I feel powerless to help."

"You can help me get into my bathing suit, the backstraps are hard to lace."

He tied the strings on her form-fitting red bathing suit and whistled when she turned around. "You are looking luscious!"

"Maybe I'll feel luscious when we get out into the sun."

They walked outside with their mugs. Jax hugged the kids, then arranged their little swim caps and tied towels around their necks like superhero capes. They ran off, towels fluttering in the breeze behind them, crying, "Nana nanana nanana Batman!"

"My little superheroes," she said. "Did you see Miranda put on her mermaid tiara?"

"She said something about having a mermaid party with the inflatable frog."

"Oh my God, she's too damn cute." Jax shook her head, smiling.

"They make us look like an all-American family. But cuter than most."

"We are an all-American family," she said.

"Of course, we are, dear. All-American Kinky."

"That's right, mock me while I'm still half-asleep." He laughed and squeezed her hand as they stared at the kids splashing around the pool. "I don't remember ever having that much fun as a child."

"Me neither," his wife said.

Cory refilled her coffee mug. "They're beautiful kids."

"I wouldn't go that far," she said, but she squeezed his hand back. "They are."

She sank into the lounge chair and sighed. The deck bowed out over the backyard with a short, open staircase that led right onto the pool area. Life was beautiful when you had a home and a family. She hated being a cliche, but now she understood why people felt that way. Happy kids. Loving husband. A nice house in a nice neighborhood. No more world war outside their windows, just trees and mountains.

She finished stretching out her body. Suddenly, she didn't feel good.

"I'll be right back, bathroom," she hurriedly explained,

getting up and going back inside the house.

When she sat on the toilet, she wanted to scream. The doctor told her not to worry, but it felt like a baby was trying to carve its way out of her abdomen with a butcher knife, only there was no baby because she wasn't pregnant, she had her period. She began panting from the pain but waited it out until she was calm enough to go back out. She put on sunglasses so Corey wouldn't see her red eyes.

She walked stiffly to her chair, trying to look less disabled and more dignified. Corey was hyper-focused on cleaning crumbs off the buffet table. He was so lost in thought, he almost didn't notice her return. She plopped down on the lounge chair with a deep sigh of relief.

"You okay?" he called to her without looking up from his crumbs.

"I'm fine, just overdid it a little last night." She put her hand on her belly. It was bloated and the pain still throbbed.

She had to get out of herself so she stared at Corey, trying to focus on him. What was he thinking about as he fastidiously cleaned? He got like that sometimes, so consumed with a task he barely noticed the world around him. Maybe he was planning his next sculpture. His muse came back to life a few months before they left New York. So did his sex drive. She was struck by the irony that, no sooner had she boasted to Carmen of Corey's libido than he had turned asexual on her. He stopped initiating. He deflected or sulked when she tried. The sudden lack of interest worried her.

But then he made his best piece yet, the sculpture in basswood which he titled "The Long Journey Home." He invited some artist friends to come by, word spread, and suddenly Corey was hot again -- in the art world and in bed. She understood. No art, no fucky.

Dry spells never seemed to slow Grandpa Paul down. But then he drank. He drank a lot. She remembered the time she got absolutely trashed with him, after Steve died. Once she had sobered up she hated herself for being so self-destructive, but now looking back at it, nostalgia softened the memory. Now it was something she and Paul had gone through together, a grief-stricken voyage to the abyss with only each other for comfort. She wished he was here with her now. He would see what a fine young man Zane was becoming, and he would meet her little angel, Miranda.

She swallowed some pain pills the doctor prescribed. It would take a while for them to kick in. Now that Corey was horny again, she was the problem. The belly pain made sex almost impossible, even between periods. She didn't tell Corey how bad sex felt but he sensed it and backed off, to both her relief and disappointment. She couldn't live like this. She hoped the doctor would have good news, but she doubted it. Deep down inside, she had a gnawing feeling that just when everything was working beautifully, perfectly, she was going to die. She was the tragic heroine of her own life story. She hated herself for being so melodramatic, but she was that way. Poor Corey, she thought. He often called her his tower of power, but right now she felt like his mountain of misery.

Her eyes darted to the pool. The kids were shrieking. Miranda was mercilessly beating Zane with a pool noodle. Zane did nothing to defend himself, laughing saying, "Help! Help!" as he tried to evade her frenzied maneuvers.

"Goddammit. Corey, do you see that?"

"Miranda's already taking after her mother, I see."

"That's not funny."

"It kind of is."

"Why isn't Zane fighting back? There's another noodle in

the pool." She waved to Zane, but he was too engrossed in evading his sister. "I mean, they can't get hurt with noodles, but still, I don't want her to think she can just beat up boys without them fighting back."

"I don't fight back," he said. "Not anymore."

"Oh. My. God. Don't even..."

"Maybe he takes after me."

"No. Stop that! Should we call them to come out?"

"Nah, let her keep beating him. It's good exercise."

"No, it isn't!"

"It builds moral character."

"No, it most certainly does not!" Why was he teasing her when this was a real problem? A terrible problem.

He saw the look in her eyes and turned serious. "They're just playing, honey. If you make a big deal out of it, they'll wonder why."

That rationalization made some sense. She leaned back in the chair, disgruntled.

"Whatever. If they grow up kinky, it'll be all your fault."

He laughed. "You're kidding, right?"

She shrugged and slumped back down into the chair. The pain had subsided, but her stress was through the roof. Maybe talking would help distract her.

"Do you miss Pro-Domming?" she asked.

"Ha! That came out of nowhere. Interesting question." He put down his crumb scraper. "I did, at first. I liked the incredible weirdness of it, and I loved seeing how people reacted. Some of them were so grateful. It boosted my ego at a time when I was fucking drowning, as you know."

"I know." She nodded. Now she was the one drowning. But she couldn't, shouldn't, wouldn't let him know how dark she felt inside. It would only frighten him.

"At the time, it made me feel useful and that was so meaningful to me. Plus I learned something new with every client and it felt like I was growing on a lot of different levels. Still, once my muse returned, I needed to sculpt and focus on my beautiful wife and kids. I think I made the right choice."

"You definitely made the right choice. I guess it took me a lot longer to get to that point, but at a certain point, fulfilling other people's fantasies gets old."

"Right? But while I was into it, it was magical. My clients made me feel like I was healing the world, one person at a time. And, of course, the fun that came with the learning, the humor of it all, the passion."

"I feel that," she said. "I remember what that was like, before it became more like a job than a passion. My first ten years at the club were like an education in life I never even knew existed. But then..."

"Exactly. It started to feel like play was real work, while art always felt like play, no matter how many hours I put into it."

He went back to cleaning up the buffet and she closed her eyes, lost in thought.

It was fun to look back on her 20s. Every day she had lived as the legendary, ass-kicking Mistress Amazon, Dominatrix deluxe, she had learned powerful, transformative lessons. How to be Dominant and sadistic, but above all, ethical and compassionate. How to let things go by leaning into your higher power and your passions. She learned how quickly some people surrender their power -- and the treacherous perils of exchanging that power with the wrong person. How wildly different people were -- not so much on the surface as in the personal details. And how to let go of things -- and people, and their choices -- that she could not control.

She had lived. LIVED. All capitals. She'd seen and done things others couldn't even comprehend. Yet, as she edged closer to 50, she knew that there were still realms she'd never explored, despite her curiosity about them. Would she ever get to explore them? Maybe not. Not now. She had to accept that no one person can visit every realm. The realm she chose now was her family, her safe harbor in life. She never wanted it to end. Ever! And especially not too soon. No, not too soon. She couldn't stand that. She HAD to see her children grow up.

"I love you," she blurted to her husband. "I love our life together."

"Oh, what brought that on?"

"Do you love our life?"

"I do."

"How much?"

"As much as the desert loves rain."

"Ahhh, nice one."

This was the weekend she needed and wanted, the kind of weekend she had dreamt of having since she first decided to move everyone to Colorado. A simple, sweet life with the people she loved. With most of the Leather Family now living in the vicinity, their home had become a hub of activity. Life was a whirl of frequent visits, frequent dinner guests, and more socializing than ever before. And it all worked! That was the most amazing part of all. They all got along.

This weekend was extra special. The whole family had gathered, along with a couple of new people Leon had met. Faint noises from the house told her that the guests were waking up and enjoying the breakfast goodies Corey set up for them in the kitchen. It was like their own mini-BDSM convention! Everyone had moved into their place for the weekend. It was glorious.

She only wished Carmen and Lo would find jobs in Denver so they could move, too. Their monthly visits were slowing down as their summer calendar was filling up. They promised to get here permanently by Christmas. That left behind Mariangela and Dane. Her brow furrowed.

"Carmen and Lo are setting up job interviews in Denver, did I tell you?"

"Already? Wow, those two work fast. I didn't realize Carmen's career was portable. I thought she was dependent on the New York art scene."

"No more than you," Jax answered. "As you said, there is art outside of New York and some of it is better than what is in New York."

"Truth," Corey said. He had been astonished by the buzz his move to Colorado received in the local art press. Just before leaving New York his boat statue was featured prominently in a gallery show. He even got some glowing reviews, which he begged Jax to read to him in bed every night that week.

"A dazzling chaos of abstract forms, hyper-realism and neo-expressionism harnessed into a stirring tribute to the voyage of life," one critic wrote.

"A must-see masterwork by a master sculptor," concluded another.

"Read that one again," Corey said.

She read it to him four more times and then they fucked like animals. She opened her eyes again to watch him work.

"I always hoped Mariangela would have what we have," she said.

Corey put down his crumb cleaner. "Uh-oh."

Mariangela had eloped with her client to Vegas to get married by Elvis. It was hilarious, though Jax was a little hurt Mariangela didn't want a formal wedding. When she got back from Vegas, Jax planned a surprise party for the newlyweds.

Mariangela was touched by the party, but the real surprise was on Jax. The minute she met Dane, she knew exactly who he was. She wanted to throw up. It was Booker's old boyfriend, the guy she drove in the cab. She may have forgotten his name, but she never forgot a face. Dane. Plain Dane. That was 100% him! How the fuck did Mariangela end up with Booker's old boyfriend?? It was a level of fucked up synchronicity she did not understand.

After toasts, when the crowd was chatting in small groups and hovering around the food table, she elbowed her way over to Dane.

"May I speak with you privately?"

"Oh!" he glanced at Mariangela. She nodded to him and waved permission. "Yeah, sure. You're Mistress Jax, the head of the family, right? I guess I... well I feel honored."

She squinted at him. Why did he look so nervous? And how dare he act as if they'd never met? What kind of game was he playing? She led him to the back of the room, where music muffled their conversation.

"I believe you and I have met before," she said. "You don't remember?"

"Really? No way! Mariangela is the first Pro-Domme I ever saw! Professionally, I mean. I mean, I never paid for it before. I mean... I hope that didn't sound as bad as I think it did." His hands shook. "Where did we meet?"

Her blood boiled for reasons she didn't even understand.

He was the guy who betrayed Booker, the fake gay guy, or maybe he was gay and wanted to prove that he wasn't by marrying Mariangela.

She scowled. "I was the cab driver who picked you up near a BDSM club and drove you back to Booker's place about 14 years ago."

"Oh my God," he screeched. "Oh my God, Jax! That Jax! Booker talked about you all the time. But he described you so differently from the way Mariangela described you that I never connected the dots." He wagged his head. "You know, Booker called you an angel, the sweetest girl he knew, while Mariangela made you sound really tough and super Dominant!"

How dumb was he? Jax's voice was as dry and crisp as a wheat thin. "I didn't see you at Booker's last party. How come?"

"I stopped going to his parties after I moved out. I didn't know he died until I bumped into his friend Raymond again at Lincoln Center a couple of years ago."

"Raymond. I know him," she said. She remembered him vaguely. He was a shy gay violinist Booker loved for a minute and then kept around for no reason he ever explained. What was it with Booker and misfits? Was she just the first in a large collection of weirdos and lost souls?

"Booker was such a good man. I'll always love him. I could never in a million years have guessed when I met him that he could end up killing himself. Never. He was such a force of Nature! Everyone loved him."

Jax didn't know whether to trust Dane's words. Lots of psychos tell stories that make them out to be saints.

"So if you loved him so much, why did you leave?"

Dane looked sad. "Well. Long story. Short version: when Booker's marriage plans with his fiancé imploded, Booker really went downhill. Like BAD."

Jax caught her breath. She didn't know about the fiancé. Booker was always falling in love and planning to marry this one or the other and none of it ever went anywhere. She didn't realize he'd gotten formally engaged. What else didn't she know? Or didn't remember? Or didn't pay attention to in the first place?

"I thought you were his long-term boyfriend."

"Oh no, no, no," Dane said. "He wasn't my boyfriend. I mean, we weren't lovers. We messed around a little, but he actually kind of rejected me for being bisexual." He gazed into her eyes. "You know, he was not BDSM at all. I mean, maybe if he was, something might have developed... but he wasn't and I was."

She already knew that. All too well. "Downhill, how?"

"Oh God." He sighed dramatically. "I hate to tell you, but Books started taking pills, snorting coke and much, much worse. You know, injecting and huffing. It was horrifying. Then he started bringing home junkies and street thugs who stole stuff and sold it for drugs. He didn't even care. Then he stopped cooking. He said it was a waste of his time to cook when you could order pizza -- and possibly get the pizza boy too."

"What?!" She couldn't believe it. Was Dane making this all up? She'd been cherishing the memory of a much loftier Booker, one who exulted in preparing gourmet meals, who cautiously pre-screened potential partners and pursued men of emotional depth and gentle manners. The Booker that Dane described was a stranger.

"I begged him to get help after one of his tricks stole my laptop," he said sadly. "Booker blamed me for leaving my room unlocked. After that, I couldn't even talk to him, it was just too sad. He said if I couldn't accept his lifestyle, I needed to go. So I found another place and moved out. He never answered my calls after that."

Again, Jax shrank inside. If what Dane was saying was true, she really didn't know the man Booker had grown up to be. It seemed impossible he could change like that. But there were signs. If she was being honest with herself, she had suspected he was either drunk or drugged when he called her to go pick Dane up. He wasn't rational that night. He just talked and talked without listening to a word she said. He even tried to bribe her to come back into his life. That wasn't who Booker was, paying people to love him. She didn't want to believe it, but as Dane told her the whole story, she couldn't help wondering if that was always who Booker was -- always thinking that he could buy love by throwing enough money at someone. Until this moment, she'd never seen him that way, but it fit the facts. That upset her even more.

"Does Mariangela know you're bi?" she said accusingly.

"What? Oh, of course, she knows. She said I can bring home all the sub guys I want," he grinned. "She's so cool. But I promised her I'd be monogamous. I'm a monogamous type when I'm with someone."

"Except to your ex-wife?"

"We were divorced when I met Mariangela." He looked mildly offended. "I do not cheat. It's a terrible thing to do to someone."

It was weird how she had a completely different narrative in her mind about Dane. She couldn't shake the suspicion that he was lying, but she recognized elements of truth in what he was saying.

But Mariangela seemed happy, and he was now part of the family whether she liked him or not. It still bothered her that Mariangela made Dane's membership in their clan a *fait accompli* by marrying him. But, of course, everyone had the right to marry whomever they wanted to, so she couldn't be mad at Mariangela for doing just that.

Jax opened her eyes. Corey was placing baskets of pastries and fresh fruit on the buffet table. "Raymond never got back to me, you know," she said.

"Who?"

"Booker's friend, the one Dane claimed he knew?"

"Oh, yeah, right."

"Yeah. I reached out to him after Dane told me they'd bumped into each other. I wonder why he didn't get back to me about Dane."

"Maybe he didn't remember who you were? Or who Dane was? Oh, that reminds me!" Corey got out his phone. "Dane said he'd help me with set-up."

"Let him do clean-up instead," she ordered. "I'm not ready to see his goofy face just now."

"I see. I guess you have thought up lots of nefarious theories about Dane's relationship with Booker, huh?"

"Not nefarious!" she raised her voice, but she blushed. She was busted. Some of her theories were pretty fucking nefarious, she had to admit to herself. Was Dane a caring, innocent person caught in a terrible situation? Or was he a leech who took advantage of her friend's kindness and then ran away when Booker needed him most?

"I don't trust Dane. Did you notice his voice is kind of nasal? It sounds like he's always whining."

"Jesus Christ, honey, cut him some slack!"

"I just want Mariangela to have what we have."

"Not everyone wants what we have, you know?"

"Come on, Corey. Everyone wants happiness. Even

masochists." She pointed at him.

"Har." He knelt beside her chair and rested his cheek on her stomach.

"Ow," she said, "move to my thighs. Your head is too heavy."

He quickly moved. "Are you okay, baby?"

"I'm fine."

"You sure? How bad is the pain today?"

"Don't avoid the subject. I just don't see them working out long-term."

"Maybe they will, maybe they won't. But, right now, she wants him and he wants her, and that's all that matters, right? They're both getting what they want. He was certainly the life of the play party last night. He was cheerful and knowledgeable. He made himself useful by helping me move all the heavy equipment around. And he's a good player, don't you think?"

"Assuming he isn't lying."

"Lying about what? Wow, what do you have against the guy? He's never done anything bad to you."

"No, but maybe he did to Booker."

"Come on, girl. Booker had much bigger problems at the end. Don't you remember his last party? The way he couldn't remember people's names or keep track of conversations? How many times did he spill drinks and slur his words? He was a trainwreck in motion. You saw that, didn't you? Because I sure did."

"I know, I know," she mumbled. The painful memories she had pushed out of her consciousness flooded back. She should have taken him to a psych ward that night. Instead, she played along with his pretense that he was just having fun and blowing off some steam.

The kids were playing quietly, Zane was swimming around the pool while Miranda was having a serious conversation with the inflatable frog.

"Do you think I'm projecting my own guilt onto Dane?"

Leon approached them and their conversation abruptly halted.

"I'll tell you, I love this house!" he exclaimed, sitting in the chair next to Jax. "Perfect for kids, perfect for entertaining adults, just an amazing find." He shook his head in admiration. "That Marco, he's a genius at matching people to the right houses."

The guests were all trickling onto the deck now, most of them wearing swimsuits with shirts or robes on top. It was a beautiful moment. She would never forget this moment, everyone she loved in one place, relaxed, happy, excited to be together for a three-day weekend.

Jax leaned over towards Leon and patted his hand.

"How are you feeling today, dear Leon? Your knees holding up okay?"

"Oh hell yeah." Leon extended his feet in the air to show them off. "The replacements are working great now. Those old knees weren't worth shit. You saw me kneel last night, right? I couldn't do that ten years ago!"

"That's really good, honey." She smiled.

"Take my advice. When you get to be my age, go bionic!"

"If I get to be your age," she said.

"Of course, you will!" he said. "You can't let setbacks stop you. You are indestructible."

She laughed weakly. "I wish."

"They have cures for everything these days." He gazed into

her eyes.

"No, they don't," she thought, but she just smiled back at him.

Corey stripped down to his swim trunks. Jax watched him longingly. His long, muscled legs, the back that narrowed to a V at his ass, the tufts of soft hair jutting from his chest and now beginning to creep around to his back. His sinewy arms were as chiseled as the wood he carved.

He sprinted to the pool like a teenager to join the kids and jumped in the water with a loud splash. Little Miranda hurried over to him with the pool noodle and started hitting him. He pretended to protest, just like Zane. "Help! Help!" he cried.

"Is he training her to be a Femdom?" Gigi came over to Jax, wearing a long black coverup and sandals, with Marla just steps behind her in a low-cut romper and flip flops.

"I'm not sure she needs training," Jax replied. "You should see what she does to her dolls."

"Barbie in bondage," Marla chirped. "That's what I did."

"I gave you a pair of flip flops for today, didn't I?" Jax asked Gigi. "You could fall and really hurt yourself out here in those heels."

"I'm not a flip-flopper," Gigi said. She showed off the heel of her sandal. "It's reasonably low."

"Did you get enough sleep last night?" Milli asked Jax. "You look tired."

Marco appeared by the side of her chair and kissed the top of her head. "Good morning, Milady."

"The kids woke me almost at dawn," Jax answered Gigi. "I'm surprised I didn't explode in the sunlight."

"Spring fever in Colorado," Marco said. "I know it well. You can't sleep, you get headaches, you walk around in a brain fog."

"Is that why my eyes feel so itchy?" Carmen appeared holding hands with Lo.

"Welcome to allergy season in Denver," Marco said. "It ain't Texas, but it ain't good."

As usual, Carmen looked too chic for the setting, wearing a leopard-print bikini that belonged on the French Riviera. She wore sparkly flat sandals and a thin gold chain on her left ankle.

"So none of the Femdoms will wear flip flops. Noted," Jax said.

"So how did Corey react when he saw this place?" Lo asked. She had settled between Carmen's legs on a lounge chair. "Catch me up, I've been so obsessed with finding a new job I'm totally out of the gossip loop."

"Well, at first, Corey thought that moving to Colorado was a terrible idea, that I'd miss New York too much and want to move back within the year," Jax said.

"I understand that," said Leon. "He's very East Coast Boston."

"That's my fear, actually," Carmen said. "That I'll start missing New York."

"Yeah, but I was so ready to get the hell out. Never mind the crime and the lockdown. The whole city changed. No matter where I went, I'd remember how things used to be and it bummed me out. The building where I began my career as a Pro-Domme is abandoned now. Did you know that?"

They all shook their heads no.

"The building was sold two months before COVID. The developers had to shut down the renovation and then squatters moved in, set fires, and basically trashed it. Now, they're thinking of demolishing it and putting up fancy condos."

"And so another chapter in BDSM history is erased," Leon said. "I remember when that club was the premiere venue for play parties."

"What did you expect," Gigi asked, "a memorial plaque?"

"Well, no, but you know," Leon said, "it's hard watching your history vanish."

Berry and Magenta were the last to assemble with them. By the looks of it, neither of them planned to go swimming.

"Raising kids in the city made it even worse. "

"Oh yeah, I can see that," Berry said, biting into a whole wheat donut. "I had a panic attack at Times Square. Too much of everything, you know? Too many rats in one cage. People, cars, tall buildings and criminals."

"I stay home more than I ever did and not just because of quarantine. There's an air of doom in the city," Carmen said. "Like maybe this is the perfect time to start a new life in a safer place."

"You did the right thing, Jax," Mariangela said. "The kids come first."

"Will you come too?" Lo asked hopefully. "It would make my Ma'am happy, I know."

"It certainly would," Carmen said. "If the whole family lived here, I could live here."

"We're thinking about it," Mariangela said.

Dane came up behind her and gave her a little hug. "I grew up in the country. It was the best part of my childhood, tromping through fields and coming home with rocks and worms in my pocket."

"Eeeeeuw!" Lo squealed. "No! Worms! EUW."

"Worms are our friends," Magenta said emphatically.

"Worms are not our friends!" Leon cried. "You know what they do to dead people."

"No, they are," Magenta said. "They aerate the soil. They consume waste. They eat..."

"OK, enough," Gigi said. "We know what they eat."

They all looked anxiously at Jax.

"If my Ma'am is ready to leave New York, I'm ready," Dane said, cutting the tension. "I had my New York experience. I'm ready for trees and open skies and breathable air."

"Exactly! That's what I told Corey. I was ready for something better," Jax continued her story. "He couldn't believe I'd ever leave New York. He kept saying things like, 'I just don't see you in overalls, darling,' and, 'Will you change your name to Farmer Jax next?'"

"What did you say?"

"I didn't argue. I knew he'd understand when he saw the house." She swept her arm and said, "I mean, who wouldn't love this? The day he finally saw the place he said, 'Fuck you're right.'" She smiled. "So I told him I am always right."

"Oh, I love that," Lo said. "You put him in his place!" She jostled Milli. "Right, baby? Nothing like a firm Femdom to put a sub in their place." Milli giggled.

"When I saw the studio, I knew Corey would be in heaven," Marco said proudly. "It's not every day you find an art studio in a private home, especially one so spacious."

"You were so right," Jax cooed.

It turned out to be the gift of a lifetime for her husband, and for her. The look on his face was a life-raft for her during stormy times. She'd never forget that moment.

"What's this, what's this?!" Corey whispered, his eyes so

wide she thought he'd faint.

"Your new studio!" she cried ebulliently. "Look how big it is! And how well-lit!"

His voice was hushed. "This is at least 3 or 4 times as big as my place back home! And the ceilings!" They were 12 feet high and had a ceiling skylight. One wall was all glass with a view of distant mountains.

"Oh my God, the light." He stood under the skylight and raised his arms toward the heavens. He never looked more beautiful to her. "The light, Jax! Can you imagine 'The Long Journey Home' standing right here, on a properly tall pedestal, in this light? The gleam of the wood? No gallery can give you the real color of sunlight."

* * *

Suddenly her phone rang, waking her from her memory. Jax checked the number. "I need to take this!" She jumped to her feet and ran back into the house, phone in hand. Her family watched her leave as if they might never see her again. They scattered into small, tearful circles and held hands.

"This is Jax," she said into the phone when she was out of hearing range. There was a tremble in her voice. Would it be Stage 4 cervical cancer? "Is this about my results?" she said as calmly as she could.

"Jax," a man's voice said, "this is Dr. Newsome."

"Brad!" She didn't expect the oncologist to be on the other end. Was he going to tell her it was all over? To come in tomorrow for emergency surgery and start chemo after that? Was he announcing her death sentence?

"Got news for me?" She tried to sound normal. She had

never been this scared. She couldn't die now. Not now. Not at this new beginning. Not when there were so many dreams still ahead. Seeing her husband finally get the acclaim he deserved, being there when her children got married, walking with them down the aisle and experiencing the joy of having grandchildren.

But. What if she had served her purpose in life? She had achieved her mission to get the children to a safe refuge and to gift her husband a private art paradise. Maybe that was what her life had been for. Maybe she was at the end of the road. It seemed so unfair. Her 50th birthday was only a few months away.

"I have good news," the doctor said, "which is why I wanted to give it to you myself as quickly as possible. You don't have cancer."

Jax almost fainted. She knelt onto the floor and hunched over her phone, rocking back and forth. "Oh my God, oh thank God, oh thank you!"

"Sorry for the delay. With this COVID thing, lab resources have slowed to a crawl. So I didn't want to make you wait another day. I got them this morning. Everything looks good. You have fibroid tumors. That's what's causing all the pain. Don't worry, they're benign. We can talk about treatment options when I see you."

"Fibroids? What are those?"

"Painful, but not fatal, inconveniences and certainly nothing you need to worry about today, Jax," he said. "I heard through the grapevine that there's a weekend party at your house."

She was so relieved she didn't know what to do with herself.

"Oh! Marco spilled the beans!" She could breathe again. The pain didn't feel as bad now that the stress drained out of her. Oh my God, she wasn't going to suffer through cancer or leave her children without a mother!!!

"We're having a Leather Family Reunion," she blurted exuberantly.

"Ah. Well, that's different."

She suddenly realized that Marco may never have told the doctor that he was kinky. She hoped the doctor wouldn't judge. "We'd love to have you and your husband over for a celebration dinner with Marco."

"Thanks! I'd love that," Brad said. "Put in a good word for me with Marco -- we really need to get moving on a new house."

"Oh I will, I will. You don't know... these past weeks... oh my God, Dr. Newsome, you just gave me back my life! Thank you, oh my God, thank you. You are the best!"

He chuckled. "Aw, thank you! This was the kind of news I love to give my patients. Gerry will contact you about a follow-up appointment, so enjoy your weekend and... whip up a little fun."

"Oh God, Brad, I love you, thank you."

She ended the call and stared at her belly. "You're not going to kill me yet, you fat bastard," she said to her belly button. She smacked it and grunted, then drew herself up tall. Proud.

She rejoined her family, squinting at the sunny skies like a prisoner stepping out of the prison gates for the first time in 20 years.

Corey, Marco, Carmen and Gigi were standing together, waiting tensely. She ran to them grinning and made the victory sign. Their relief was palpable.

"You're going to be okay?" Marco asked. "Please, girl, don't keep us waiting!"

"I'm going to be okay," she said. Repeating it in a loud voice, "I AM OKAY!"

Corey reached his hand out, almost afraid to touch her. She grabbed it and put it to her lips, kissing the palm.

"I am! I'm okay! No cancer! No cancer at all. Marco, thank you for getting me in with Dr. Newsome. He's amazing. That was him on the phone. He called me personally. How many doctors do that these days?! On a Sunday!!"

"I told him you were my sister. He knew he was not getting a house with me unless he treated you as the Queen you are." Marco hugged her and picked her up to swing her around. He was exuberant. "I have to go tell the boys, they've been praying hard for you. Love ya, darling."

"Love you, too," she said. "Love you all! Thank you! I'm sorry I worried you so much."

"Sister Darling, I knew you'd be okay, I just knew it in my heart." Carmen was in her arms next. "I couldn't lose you. I just couldn't."

"Aw, Carmen, don't cry." They hugged for an eternal minute, kissing each other's cheeks. Jax dried Carmen's tears with her fingers. "I'm going to be fine, sweetheart, it's all good now."

"Well, that's a fucking relief!" Gigi said. "I'm not a hugger, but let me tell you I almost shit myself when the phone rang."

"That's Ma'am's way of saying she loves you very much," Milli joked.

Gigi slapped her ass.

"Shut up, Milli. And, Leon, stop crying. Jesus Christ. It's good news! Come on, boy, pull yourself together," Gigi said.

"We better tell the youngers." Milli nudged Leon and found a tissue for him in her pocket so he could blow his nose.

"The youngers have been burning incense, casting runes, and playing tarot, and that bullshit has to stop," Gigi cackled. "I love you, Jax! Thank God you're okay!"

"Go! Go! Love you all! Now go, tell everybody. I am alive and well and going to be with you, well, right now I'm planning on forever!"

After the crowd dissipated, Corey finally took her in his arms.

"So you'll be okay?" He needed more assurance.

"Pretty much, yeah. It's something called fibroids. The doctor said if I can tough out the pain, it will probably resolve on its own when I hit menopause. I'll do a follow-up to see what kind of treatments they offer. Worst case, I'll need a hysterectomy, but Brad said probably not."

"Oh, my God. Is it safe to have sex???"

"I like your priorities," she said.

Now he got emotional. "I don't know how I'd live without you, I don't." He buried his face in her hair. "Life wouldn't be worth living." His big heart was pounding so hard they made her shoulders shake.

"It's okay, baby. You won't have to live without me, see? I'll be here to torment you for years to come." She glanced around happily, looking for the kids. "Where's Miranda?"

"In the pool."

"No, she isn't. Where did she go?"

Corey pulled away to slowly scan the pool. Zane was floating on his back, but their little girl was nowhere in sight. "Where is she?" he muttered. They hurried back to the buffet area.

"Has anyone seen Miranda? Did she get out of the pool?" she called out to them.

"No, I haven't seen her. Wasn't she in the pool?" they called back.

She and Corey ran to the edge of the deck. "Miranda," they shouted. "Miranda! Where are you? Miranda!"

Jax's blood turned to ice. Not this. Not now. Not on this day when her own life was given back to her! It couldn't be happening. It was happening. It couldn't be.

"Why did you leave them alone?!" she screeched at Corey. "Why? You know they have to be supervised."

"I swear I kept my eye on her," he said. "I swear, right up until we started hugging. It couldn't have been more than 30 seconds. Oh my God. It is all my fault. MIRANDA!" he bellowed.

"I'm sorry, I shouldn't have said that. It's not your fault," she apologized. "I'm so rattled." But her mind raced, imagining one catastrophe after another. Miranda ran away. She was kidnapped. A mountain lion attacked her!

In seconds, everyone was racing around, screaming and calling for the child. Leon and Milli ran toward the tree line in case she'd wandered into the woods. Marco and his partners ran to the front of the house in case she had wandered there. Carmen and Lo ran into the house, shouting her name.

Mariangela grabbed Corey's arm. "Where was the last place you saw her?"

"She was in the pool with Zane. She had her mermaid crown on and was talking to the inflatable frog. I swear, I only looked away for a minute! A single minute!"

"Dane," Mariangela ordered, "the pool. NOW."

"OH MY GOD!" both parents shrieked at the same time. What if their baby had drowned? Jax got tunnel-vision and half-closed her eyes. Her daughter had drowned. No, no, no. This couldn't be happening. Not to her baby daughter. No. She was playing somewhere, she had to be, she had to be. She galloped blindly to the pool behind her husband.

"Zane! Zane!" she screamed. "Get out of the pool right now! Zane!"

Out of the corner of her eye, a pasty white shadow in a pink speedo flew by. It was Dane, running so fast he left them in the dust like he was Usain Bolt. Before she could catch her next breath, Dane dove into the pool and vanished under the surface.

Those next seconds opened like a chasm. Time stopped. It was a living nightmare. It just couldn't be happening. No. She'd had a vision of death. But the death she had foreseen wasn't coming for her, it had come to take her daughter!! What was Dane doing down there? Did he find her? Why wasn't he coming back up? It was taking too long. Her baby was dead! Maybe Dane was trapped in whatever had sucked her into the pool's depth. She couldn't live without her baby girl. Her world would end.

With a loud splash, Dane surfaced, holding what at first appeared to be a deflated pool toy. He swam back to the side of the pool and gently placed it on the concrete before hoisting himself out of the water.

Jax stared dizzily at the tiny figure. It was a toy she didn't recognize, pale gray and wearing Miranda's bathing suit. Jax screamed.

"My baby!" the parents howled in unison. "My little baby girl, no, no, no, no..."

Jax and Corey circled the tiny body, shrieking her name, as if trying to summon her back from death. Mariangela intercepted them.

"Let Dane do this," Mariangela said. "Let Dane. He knows what to do, let him."

Dane crouched over the child and began performing resuscitation while the parents watched in terror.

Dane worked on her and worked on her. It took so long. Every second lasted ten minutes. Corey and Jax clung to each other, crying and moaning.

There was a tiny wet cough. Then another bigger, wetter one. Miranda spat out water and choked.

"Thatta girl," Dane said softly. "Good girl. You'll be okay, honey." He lightly stroked her hair. He motioned to Jax that it was okay now to take over. He walked a few steps away and collapsed on the ground, shaken and exhausted.

"I knew you could do it, I knew you could." Mariangela got on her knees and comforted him. "You saved her! I'm so proud of you."

"Holy fuck," he whispered. "Holy fuck. I never saved anyone's life before." He threw his arms around his wife and sobbed into her chest.

"You're a good man, Dane," she consoled him. "You're a wonderful man."

Miranda's eyes popped wide open. She looked up innocently at her parents as if nothing had happened.

"Am I a mermaid now, Mommy?" She looked down at her legs. "Where is my tail?"

"What are you talking about? What do you mean, baby?"

"Mr. Frog said if I sat on the bottom and waited long enough, I'd grow a tail instead of legs and then I'd be a mermaid."

"What?! You sat down?? Oh, my gawwwwd! I can't... even," she sobbed.

"Oh, honey, no, we don't sit underwater," Corey said, half

laughing and crying at the same time.

The whole family surrounded them now, anxiously peering at the child. They'd all put their robes back on out of some kind of odd sense of respect.

"Miranda! Jax, what happened?? Did she fall and hit her head?" they cried out.

"She wanted to be a mermaid, so she sat down on the bottom of the pool waiting for her tail to grow," Corey said in shock, slapping his hand to his forehead. "So she could be a mermaid."

Everyone was stunned. Lo was crying. "Our baby, our baby, we almost lost our baby girl," she wailed. "I should've been watching her!"

Carmen comforted Lo by saying, "It's okay now, beauty, it's okay, she's going to be okay."

"Holy fuck," Gigi finally said. "Did she black out?" Her whole body shuddered. "Thank God Dane got to her so fast."

"Damn, that boy can swim!" Carmen said.

"Holy fuckamole," Wesley said, blinking back tears. "Wow. This is why I don't want kids."

Jax took her daughter gently into her arms, cradling her, cooing at her as if she was still a baby, so careful with the precious little body, the fragile limbs, the tiny bones.

"Mommy loves you so much, Mommy loves you so, so much." She rained kisses on her child's face.

"Would you love me more if I was a mermaid, Mommy?"

"No, baby, no, I love you just the way you are. You are perfect to me."

"But I want to be a mermaid." She hiccupped and another mouthful of water spilled out.

"How would we go shopping, though?" I'd have to wheel you around in a giant fish tank and it wouldn't fit through the doorway."

"Well, that's not right," the little girl said thoughtfully. "Life isn't fair, is it, Mommy?"

"No, darling," Jax hugged her close, "it isn't."

Zane stood next to them, completely lost. "What happened to Miranda?"

Corey steered him away to talk about it.

What a fucking day! Everything she'd ever learned about life flashed through Jax's mind. The emotional highs and lows, the traumas you get over and the ones you never recover from, the good days and the bad days and the horrible, hair-wrenching days.

She had to get back to reality for everyone's sake. She needed to breathe and focus on **here** and **now**. In the here and now, they were all together. They were all alive. She, her daughter, and Gigi, all of them were skating at the edge of death, but at such different stages of life and in such different ways.

A few feet away, Dane was still recovering. The man had saved her daughter's life! After all the criticism, mistrust, and ugly thoughts she'd felt, now she felt only shame and regret for treating him so coldly.

"Thank you for saving my baby's life," she called to him. "I will never forget what you did. Never. In saving her you saved me, my husband, and my son, all of us, even our friends and family. You're my hero now, Dane. I will always be grateful to you. Thank God you are in our family."

Dane got so flustered at the spate of praise he couldn't speak.

"Little known fact. Dane was a lifeguard in college," Mariangela beamed. "I knew if anyone could save her, he could." She patted him on the head. "And he did."

Dane looked like he'd been to hell and back. Maybe he had. Maybe there were a lot more layers to Dane than Jax gave him credit for.

"Thank you, Ma'am. I'm glad I could prove to the family that I can be useful," he finally said.

Corey and Zane returned from their talk. Zane broke away from his father and ran to his mother.

"You're a good, sweet boy," she said, then kissed the top of his head.

"I didn't protect her, Mom." He wept. "It was my job."

"No, it wasn't, honey, no it wasn't. It's all Mr. Frog's fault. You're a great brother. And the only thing that matters is that we are all safe." She kissed him, then she kissed Miranda and when Corey joined them, she covered him with kisses too.

"Will you punish Mr. Frog?" Miranda asked. "He is a bad frog."

"Yes he is!" they all agreed.

"Will you punish him? Punish him!" the little girl said in a weird voice.

"Don't worry." Corey picked her up and held her tightly. "Mr. Frog is no longer welcome here. I'm going to banish him so he can never lie to you again."

* * *

That night, after the children were dried off and fed and tucked into bed, the adults retreated to the concealed dungeon in their basement. Berry stayed upstairs to keep an eye on their kids and all the dogs everyone brought with them. Berry decided that watching the kids and rolling around on the floor with eight cuddly dogs would be his biggest joy in life, so everyone shrugged and agreed it was a good idea for someone to stay upstairs that night. They'd been through enough that day.

Corey placed a huge bowl of fruit punch on a table.

"What? No vodka? What kind of fruit punch is this?" Lloyd was dismayed.

"BDSM fruit punch," Leon whispered. "We don't drink when we play."

"Aw, geez, after the day we had? I can't." He pulled a flask out of his pocket and poured a double shot into his plastic glass. "L'Chaim," he said to himself.

Leon grabbed the flask and poured a shot into his glass. "Mazel Tov."

"A toast to milady!" Corey held up his glass. "The best wife, the best mother, the best Leather sister, the best friend and the best Sadist I've ever known."

"The best therapist money can't buy," Carmen called out.

"The best work-wife in the world," Marco offered.

"The best daughter a woman could hope for," Gigi said with emotion.

"The best frighteningly efficient woman I know," Leon said, making everyone guffaw.

They raised their glasses to her.

Jax was embarrassed and humbled by their words. This moment was everything. She looked around at her friends' beautiful faces. Everyone she loved was in her house. Everyone was safe. Everyone loved each other. It was a miracle.

"So..." she said as she looked around, "is it time?"

"Oh, it's definitely time," Corey said.

"Boys, it's time!" Marco said. "Go get our surprise now."

Leon turned to Jax. "They brought something real special for you."

"Very special!"

Lloyd and Wesley left the dungeon and returned fifteen minutes later carrying two enormous bags, which they set carefully on the ground.

"Let me help you with that." Corey ran over to them.

"What's in the bag, what's in the bag?" everyone asked curiously.

"That, my friends," Marco said, "is a one-of-a-kind spanking bench." He looked at Jax. "It's fit for a Queen."

"Look, darling," Corey said to her, "check this out!"

The men stepped back so everyone could see the finished bench.

True enough, it was a one-of-a-kind spanking bench. Jax knew the minute she saw it that it was Corey's work. The vertical post had an ornate crown carved at the top. It matched the engagement ring box Corey once made for her, and her name was engraved and filled with gold.

"Oh my God," she said.

"Oh my God," everyone else said. "It looks so solid. What kind of wood did you use?"

Corey puffed up proudly and replied, "It's black walnut. And look," he said as he showed them the features, "stocks for wrists and a seat wide enough for the fattest ass!"

Milli cracked up. "Oh, so you made it for me."

"No, he clearly made it for me," Lo said. They pretended to box with each other over who got to use it first.

"As the eldest sub, I deserve that privilege!" Leon bent over laughing.

"Everyone will get their turn, don't worry," Jax called to them.

"Plus, look," Corey said as he showed them a wide side compartment. It contained several new paddles. "You can store toys right here. How's that for convenience!"

"It's exquisite," Jax said, then ran her hands over the smooth wood. "Finest piece of equipment I've ever seen, darling!" She ran up to Corey and hugged him gently. "I love it."

Then she whispered, "I'm saving that for you. I want you to be the first one to be bound to it. It will be the highlight of the night. You'll put on a show for us that no one will ever forget."

"Yes, my Queen," he shivered, instantly aroused.

While the others oohed and aahed over the bench, Jax went to the whip collection hanging on a wall rack and selected a toy she called the "Angry Whip" because it was heavily braided in red leather. According to Corey, the lashes burned like fire.

"Oh, not that one," they whispered among themselves. "Shouldn't you start with something softer?" they asked.

"No," she said haughtily. "Not tonight. I'm celebrating. So who's the first?"

Everyone turned to Corey. "Corey will be the last one tonight! Also the first to break in the spanking bench."

The crowd stirred in agitated delight. "Oh, yeah," they murmured, "that's sweet, so romantic."

Mariangela poked Dane in the ribs. "Go on, wimp, raise your hand, it's an honor."

Jax fixed her cold gray eyes on the newlyweds. "Dane? Your Mistress just volunteered you!"

Dane got shy, but Mariangela pinched him hard, so he got up and walked to the front. He was about to kneel, but Jax stopped him, putting a firm hand on his shoulder.

"Strip first," she ordered, fondling the heavy whip. Its padded leather handle felt like a fat cock in her hand, only with a pommel in place of a handle. She waved the whip as if testing it and flashed it through the air. Her audience watched her whip skills with admiration. At one point, she made the lashes appear to float in the air. Swirling and twirling it expertly, her wrist and hand moved in concert with the implement. Her hand joined with the whip handle, merging into the whip, until it looked like the whip was an extension of her body.

Dane stripped down to a red silk jockstrap with an elephant penis sheath. The ears bobbed as Dane's knees wobbled. The crowd loved that, tittering and catcalling at him: "Elephant boy!" and, "Make the trunk rise!" and, "Tusk! Tusk! Tusk!"

She tapped the trunk lightly. "Remove this ridiculous animal from your anatomy! What were you thinking, slut?"

"Well..." He was so embarrassed he almost fell while taking it off. "Mistress Mariangela made me wear it."

"I did," Mariangela said. She had moved up front to watch the action closely.

"Good choice, honey," Jax said to his Mistress. She extended her arm to gather force, and stinging kisses fell upon his naked member.

"Oh! Ooh! OW. OW. OOOOH!" he yelped as he danced on his toes.

"I see you're a shower. Are you also a grower?"

"You bet he is!" Mariangela yelled. "Why do you think I

married him!?"

"You go, girl." Wesley stood up to clap.

"Sit down, Wesley," Jax said. "You'll get yours soon enough."

Marco pulled his boy back down by his leather thong. "This isn't a drag show."

"Consider this your rite of passage into the Family," Mistress Jax said loud enough for the room to hear. "Are you ready to take 50 strokes of this whip?"

"50?" Dane was incredulous. "With THAT whip?" He appealed to his wife with his eyes. "Ma'am?"

"He's ready!" Mariangela assured Jax. "He's more than ready. Do your worst."

Dane bit his lip in terror, then met Jax's gaze. Warmth beamed from her eyes and his fear receded. She stepped towards him and tenderly wiped a line of sweat off his forehead. Her touch made him shiver. She grabbed him by the hair, pulling his head towards her, so close he could smell the sweet fragrance of her body and feel her breath on his face. Then she pushed him roughly. "Turn around," she ordered. "Your ass is my grass now."

Jax had decided she would do this with feeling, deep feeling. Today had completely changed her view of him. Her heart moved for him. He was a good guy. And he was right to flee Booker. She would have done the same. She liked her pot, but meth was a terrible drug and huffing was horrible.

He had saved her precious child's life. Her heart was finally open to Dane. Wide open. He was the right one for Mariangela after all.

And the bizarre irony of it all sank in. She was dominating Dane! It's what Booker asked for those many years ago. She was fulfilling his wish now. How crazy was that?

She leaned in and brushed Dane's ear with her lips, whispering softly, "This is what Booker wanted, for me to Dom you. But tonight, it's what I want. Thank you for giving me this opportunity."

He trembled. "Thank you, Ma'am, thank you so much. You are everything Mariangela said you were."

For a second, she stared up as if the ceiling had opened and shown her the skies. Closure. Dane was giving her closure on Booker. It was another unexpected blessing he had now brought into her life. She had a place for him in her heart after all, a special place that sealed their future as friends. She felt humbled, grateful. "Thank you for saving my daughter's life. Thank you."

His eyes glittered with submission. "Thank you, Ma'am." He sighed. "I'm so happy now."

And so it began as it always did. A hush fell over the watchers. Jax slowly raised the whip to bring it down with vicious exactitude on Dane's ass. Jax laced Dane's buttocks and thighs with a fury of pale pink streaks that turned crimson. She was unrelenting, but not unmerciful. She leaned in after every series of strokes to check on Dane, to ensure she was not taking him beyond his capacities, and giving him the strength to take even more.

Corey walked to the front to watch their scene close up, mesmerized by his Goddess. His wife, who only a few hours ago had thought she was dying, whose own child had nearly died that day, had risen like a tower of indomitable strength.

Corey sank to his knees. She was herself once more -- focused, purposeful, completely in charge. As Dane whimpered and screamed, Jax turned her head to Corey and mouthed, "I love you." He swooned with desire. She beckoned him closer and he crawled to her side. She pulled Corey close until his face was buried in her left thigh. Her pain was gone. Her eyes glowed with triumph.

Her ship had come home and she was its captain. She had sprung back to life and would stay alive for years to come! Her husband clasped her legs, in the pose he'd so dexterously memorialized in his statue. Yes, she was home now.

She inhaled sharply. "Welcome to the Family, Dane," she shouted, landing a blow that made everyone gasp. "Welcome to your home of the heart."

❧ About the Author ☙

Legendary author, sex therapist, and long-time lifestyle dominatrix, Dr. Gloria G. Brame has been a pioneer of BDSM/fetish study, education, research, and advocacy for over 30 years. She founded the first online peer support forum for kinky people on Compuserve in 1987 and published her first bestseller, *Different Loving* (co-authors, William Brame and Jon Jacobs), in 1993. Since then, Gloria's maintained a passionate  commitment to helping sexually non-conventional people overcome obstacles and find their joy. Gloria has authored 10 books in different genres to spread her gospel that sex and gender diversity is the true norm for adults. *Kink So Real* is the sequel to her award-winning novel, *Amazon Hammer*.

Gloria Brame may be contacted through her website **gloriabrame.com**, and you can follow her on Facebook, X (previously Twitter), Amazon, GoodReads, LinkedIn, Alignable, and other social platforms.